Emily

By Matthew Elstran

Published By Matthew Elstran
Chippewa Falls, Wisconsin USA
www.stayatthehideaway.com

ISBN 069296455X

Cover art by Olivia

"In the 1960's, small family resorts were at the peak of their popularity and number in northern Minnesota and Wisconsin."

The above illustration is courtesy of Tricia, a construct of the author's limited imagination.

Chapter 1   Saturday

Emily stood on the end of the dock, gazing intently at a small white object halfway across the lake. A seagull was floating lazily, its color sharply contrasting the deep blue of the water that reflected the late afternoon sky in mid August. An event from her past occupied her thoughts. Yet, one detail was missing.

Her musings were suddenly interrupted by a familiar voice, "I thought I might find you out here." Emily, turning, exclaimed, "Timothy Vincy! Is it really you!" and the two old acquaintances exchanged a friendly hug. Then with a playful reproach she said, "How have you been? You never responded to my last letter."

Tim, having not seen Emily in person for two years, felt strangely uncomfortable seeing her now, staring fixedly at him as she was. He managed an unconvincing reply, "I've been pretty busy." To which she responded, "Entertaining fashion models and movie stars in your new bachelor's quarters no doubt." She was smiling wryly but her dark brown eyes were deep and questioning. "Oh, not exactly," murmured Tim. "Adjusting carburetors and installing nitrous oxide canisters then, I suppose?" pursued Emily. "You know me too well," said Tim lightly. Then, in a more serious and quiet tone, "but I don't feel like I know you anymore. You've changed, you know what I mean?" "I am sure I do not," replied Emily, still looking steadily at Tim. She had detected a nervous tension in his voice. Then Tim, rousing his courage, said, "You've grown into a beautiful young woman."

At this, Emily shyly turned her head away and slightly downward. Her long brown hair fell across her face and Tim did not see her blush, but he sensed, correctly, that he had been misunderstood. "I mean, not the way you look," Emily turned back to him with a raised eyebrow and a smile like a flame, "well, yes you look beautiful, but I meant something else."

They both stood in awkward silence. A gust of southwest wind set an oak leaf adrift out onto the lake. Someone behind them clanged the cover off a Weber grill. A rusty swing set chain squeaked. A boat raced by pulling a skier behind.

"Do you remember when your father took you and I and Tricia out in that orange boat? We went over there, where the dam is and threw bread out for the seagulls," said Emily as she looked north. "We must have had fifty of them following us." Then, turning back to Tim, "Whose boat was that?" "1974 Lund fiberglass tri hull, " replied Tim, relieved by the change of subject. "Four cylinder GM engine, 140 horse-power, Mercruiser sterndrive." Nodding her approval, Emily said, "Yes, that's the one." Tim continued, "It was my uncle's. He sold it." "Oh," said Emily wistfully, "I would like to take my niece out to feed the seagulls."

"Is Elizabeth enjoying motherhood?" asked Tim earnestly. "It's what she's always wanted," answered Emily. "She's happy."

Emily possessed an inexhaustible treasure of facial expression and her expressions were genuine. She had lively, thin, dark, eyebrows, arched above eyes that could shift from a placid softness to a razor sharp glare with an astonishing suddenness. Her mouth and lips formed into a vast array of configurations that were expressive of even the most subtle mood change.

Tim felt as if he were peering directly at a soul unmasked, a soul that had grown to maturity without being tarnished by the sarcasm, the skepticism, the cynicism, and all the other ism's and asm's that plague civilization. A soul that had clung tenaciously to the childlike wonder, optimism, hope, that is so often lost. Indeed, it was the loss of these that Tim lamented and their return that he longed for, though, this was as yet, unclear to him.

Here was 24-year old Emily Brooke, a gemlike radiance in her cheeks, coolly confident in her world-view, at peace with her place in the universe. Her eyes, deep brown pools of contemplation, were fixed on Tim now, yet her mouth was mischievously smiling, and her tone playfully mocking as she said, "I remember when you were sweet on Beth." (Emily called her older sister Elizabeth, "Beth" while Tricia, Emily's younger sister, called Elizabeth, "Liz." This has led to no little confusion. Many alumni of their high school claim there were four Brooke sisters. I have even heard of one daring young fellow that claimed to have dated all four but I can assure you, there were only three.)

Tim smiled and changed the subject, "Is the rope swing still up?" "It was gone when we came last year," answered Emily. "The owner had to cut the tree down. It was dead."

They walked slowly, talking along the way, to where the tall cottonwood had once stood, supporting a fifty foot, one inch diameter, hemp rope, which swung out over a backwater they called the pond. All that was left was a gravestone-like stump.

As they stood mourning the loss of a favorite summer activity, something caught Emily's eye. "Look, is that a muskrat or an otter?" She was pointing to the center of concentric ripples that were spreading on the other side of the pond. "Let's follow it," she whispered.

Lying on the bank near them was an old red canoe, which had been a fixture at the resort since the 1960's. It was manufactured by Grumman, the company that made the lunar land-ing module for the Apollo 13 Space Mission.

Fourteen years earlier, the sisters Brooke, Tim, and two other similar aged revelers who were also staying at the resort that summer, would overturn this canoe in the swimming area. Then, they would duck underwater and come up underneath the upside down hull. The light coming up through the water cast an eerie glow inside and their voices would echo off the riveted aluminum walls of their capsule.

Tim and Emily had a more conventional use in mind now. Tim went to look for paddles. Emily had drug and pushed the canoe into the water by the time Tim returned empty handed. "The paddles were in the canoe already," she said as she stood impatiently on the shore, waiting for Tim to help her into the boat.

Emily needed no help getting into a canoe mind you. It was her natural expectation that a gentleman help a lady into a boat. Woven into the fabric of her upbringing, was a conviction that a women's role was to encourage civility in men. To counter men's tendency toward a more base existence, to soften the hard edge, smooth over the coarseness, to harness the raw energy of man and redirect it toward a more noble purpose, was simply the proper thing to do as a female of the species, according to her understanding. "If man has evolved from the ape," her father used to say, "there is probably a woman to blame for it."

Holding Tim's hand, Emily stepped lightly into the canoe and sat down in front. The two friends had canoed often together and maneuvered their vessel easily, following a path of bubbles, which is the sure sign of an otter. About twenty yards ahead, the otter emerged, then, another, and another, there were three! They dove and then reemerged playfully for some time, seem-ingly paying no heed to the two alien observers, but maintaining their distance just the same. Eventually, they scrambled up the bank and disappeared from sight.

Their entertainment having taken leave, the two quietly sat for a while, reflecting. Tim was watching a painted turtle push its way through some weeds nearby. Emily was focused on a particular point on the shore, a small opening between the fiddlehead ferns and the elderberry bushes. Presently she said, "Isn't that where the pomegranate seed would roll into the pool and change into a fish?" "Traitress!" cried Tim suddenly in a hoarse voice. "Did we not swear never to cross one another's path?" "Wretch!" replied Emily in her princess heroine voice, "I took no oath with thee." Then, they laughed genially at themselves.

One summer, Tim had found a copy of The Arabian Nights in his cabin. He and Emily would reenact the epic battle from the Story of the Three Calendars. She was The Lady of Beauty and he the Efrite. He had made her memorize the lines and she had loved every minute of it. After the son of Iblis was reduced to ashes, Emily would say with much drama, as she stood in a ring of stones which formed the campfire ring by Tim's cabin, "He forced me to the last test of fire and I conquered. Yet I die, for this fire cannot be quenched, except by my life."

Words convey meaning. They have the power to change the course of events. But sometimes, when viewed retrospectively, words are just sadly coincidental.

As they began to paddle again, Tim stealthily snatched the aforementioned turtle from his natural habitat and quietly introduced it to a strange, aluminum environment. He kept up a conversation so that Emily would not hear the sharp little claws scraping at the bottom of the inherently instable canoe as it crawled toward her bare feet. That conversation went like this: "Do you remember that time, collecting turtles for racing, and that turtle got snagged on your ankle bracelet? You jumped up and nearly tipped us over." "I tried to shake it off but it was just hanging on, until my bracelet broke, and they both went into the water. You fished out my bracelet and repaired it with a pair of needle nose pliers from your tackle box," said Emily dreamily.

Turtle racing was conducted as follows: Painted, also known as, Sun turtles (Chrysemys Picta) were caught from the pond or lake in sufficient quantity so as to be able to assign one turtle to each human participant. The turtles were allowed to lounge about in a galvanized steel tub, which was filled partially with water and then furnished with rocks and sticks and other such items to their liking, until the race was ready to commence. When all were ready, each person would set their turtle free in a grassy area near the old rope swing and the first turtle back to the water would be declared winner along with their human counterpart. You were allowed to shout words of encouragement but not touch or redirect your turtle in any way.

Now consider this, the sensation of a hard, wet, scratchy reptile crawling across your bare foot is a startling one, even for an experienced turtle racer. If you will further consider that their reminiscing had a lulling effect on both of them and that Tim was leaning over to observe a small fish, you will not be surprised at what happened next. The turtle had made its way to the front of the canoe and Emily's reaction was more than Tim had bargained for. The bottom of the Grumman was suddenly glistening in the afternoon sun, having deposited its three passengers into the cool green water.

Laughing, they swam to shore, pulling the canoe along with them. The sudden shock of the cold water had awakened every cell of Tim's body. His senses were suddenly acute, keenly aware, heightened to their fullest extent. He felt completely alive. Colors were vivid, sounds clear, the atmosphere electric.

They made their way to a dock, aiming to climb up in order to avoid trudging through emergent weeds. With a sudden burst of energetic gallantry, he scooped Emily up to set her on the dock.

Her wet skirt clung to her legs. The gold ankle bracelet, the same one he had repaired, sparkled in the sun. Her delicate perfume mingled intoxicatingly with the musty, earthy smell of her pond water drenched hair. He felt the warmth of her skin against his.

In the past, an appetite, a base desire, the terms of which could be set forth explicitly in a legal document, a contract, would have consumed him as if he were interacting with a mere object, exercising an exchange of goods or services. But now his conscience revolted at this desire, suggesting that it would disqualify him from being worthy of her. It was an 'other' not an

12

object, that he was attracted to, a person with inherent dignity, and in the case of Emily, a person who demanded an exchange of persons, a covenant.

An internal struggle, not uncommon, perhaps universal even, but a struggle just the same, rendered Tim confused and silent for the moment.

When two gears are properly spaced and well oiled, power is transmitted with maximum efficiency. When not, there is noise, galling, heat, and, eventually, damage.

The point where the gear of emotion and feeling meshes with the gear of intellect and will, in literature, is referred to as the human heart. Tim's gears had not been spaced with exacting precision. They needed a shim added somewhere.

His confusion went unnoticed by his enchantress, however, as she went to change into dry clothes.

The two of them met up again later. It was early evening now and Tim had kindled an inviting campfire. Emily came around with two cups of decaffeinated coffee. "I still have a chill from our unexpected swim," she said, handing Tim a cup. She was now wearing a pastel summer dress with a light sweater.

The midday temperature had been eighty degrees, but as the sun had set, the temperature had dropped off significantly.

They sat near each other in silence, staring at the mesmerizing glow of embers. The burning pine made a soothing, crackling sound as it emitted the smoky odor, which is the very essence of a Northwoods Wisconsin resort. He took a sip of coffee, a bullfrog croaked, a distant train rumbled, a wood screen door slammed shut and Tim was content in the knowledge that there was no other place in the world he would rather be at that moment than sitting next to this fascinating creature, whom he had known for much of his life, so familiar and yet so mysterious.

For her part, Emily was wondering what Tim was thinking about. It is a great curiosity that women spend so much time in that occupation.

After a few minutes of silence, her thoughts turned to the Arabian Nights and their recent reminiscent exchange, then, to another book they had read together. She asked, "Do you re-member the year that we read 'My Side Of The Mountain' to-gether? I found a copy in our cabin and we took turns reading it out loud. I don't think we finished it, but you just had to try boiling water in a leaf. I was young and impressionable at that time and I remember being affected with a very favorable opinion of your abilities." Tim smiled. He had not thought of that book for quite some time. "I remember you just had to try eating cattail roots, but I'm not sure I was impressed by that at the time. I thought it was a little strange actually."

(It's true. You can boil water in a leaf. Try it for yourself. A burdock leaf works well for this purpose. Just stitch it into some sort of pouch with a vine or flexible twig and affix it to a branch so it can be held in the flames.)

Tim and Emily sat near each other, staring at the fire, thinking about their past friendship and the status of their present relationship.

Their peaceful silence was eventually interrupted by Mr. Brooke and Tricia, "You don't happen to have a fly swatter in your cabin do you Tim?" asked Tricia as they joined the campfire vigil. She didn't really need one. She was teasing her sister.

Emily had a quirky detestation for flyswatters and toilet plungers. While she recognized their occasional utilitarian value, she maintained that they should be used discreetly then quickly hidden away in some out of the way place so their unsightly ap-pearance would not cause offense.

Tim responded, "I brought one from home. It's on the dash of my car if you want to grab it." (This was said in jest. The only item to be found on the dash of his car was a package of plastigauge, used for checking bearing clearances.)

Emily had a look on her face that said as plainly as words, "How long do I have to suffer with these mere mortals?" Harold interjected, "Seriously now Tim, how is your job going?" They talked about jobs and other matters of consequence for some time, enjoying each other's company as darkness fell over the Hideaway Resort.

Chapter 2 Sunday

In August of 1993, Harold Brooke and his family packed up half of their belongings, loaded them into their Pontiac Bonneville (3.8L V6, 4 speed automatic) and set out from their home in Milwaukee, on vacation. The "Are we there yets?" began at about Madison and continued for three hours until they reached Chippewa Falls. His wife Lorraine, when she wasn't advising Harold on his driving, read books to the three girls in the back seat: Elizabeth, who was 8 years old, Emily, 6 and Tricia, 5.

In the 1960's, small family resorts were at the peak of their popularity and number in northern Minnesota and Wisconsin. As a child, Harold had spent a week at the lake, each summer, with his family, and he wanted his girls to have the same experience. Having earned his first week of paid vacation at the foundry, Harold had tried to make a reservation at the same resort, in Hayward, that he remembered so fondly. He was disappointed to learn that it had been redeveloped into condominiums. With that option not available, he decided to try something a bit closer and settled on the Hideaway Resort on Lake Wissota.

The Hideaway was founded in 1953 by Harry and Blanche Lea. (Harry once flew his airplane underneath the Cobban Bridge. Detailing all of his exploits would require a whole other book.)

Emily got along tolerably well with her sisters, at that age, and the three of them spent the week swimming, catching frogs, making friends, climbing trees, building sand castles, telling stories around the campfire, fishing, and many other activities of that sort. At the end of the week, Harold and Lorraine made reservations to return the following summer. The girls promised to write their new friends, (but never did) packed the Bonneville full of special rocks, leaves, snail shells, driftwood, and (unknown to their parents) a large beetle and one dead toad, and drove back to the city. That was the beginning of an annual pilgrimage that had continued to the present time.

The next day was Sunday. An early morning rain had given way to a beautiful, partly cloudy afternoon. Tim found Emily, lying on a Dora The Explorer beach towel, next to a little girl. They were studying something in the grass.

As the rain had soaked into the ground, it had driven an earthworm to the surface. They watched as the segmented body felt about blindly, stretching and recoiling. This small creature had ascended from a subterranean world that was teaming with life. Worms pulled organic matter into the soil. The plants above produced exudates, which attracted fungi and bacteria to the roots below. The bacteria and fungi broke down organic material into a form that the plant roots could absorb. The bacteria and fungi were eaten by protozoa and nematodes. These were in turn eaten by micro arthropods. All of this predation built soil structure that allowed for aeration. A soil food web filled with symbiotic connectivity. In nature, relationship is everything.

"I see you've made a new friend," said Tim. "This is Lydia. She is staying with her family in the Birch this week... the haunted cabin," said Emily, adding the part about the haunted cabin with a mock resignation that her new friend's vacation was surely doomed. "I'm sorry to hear that," replied Tim as he tried to look impressively sympathetic. "Any cabin but Birch," he added.

The wide eyed Lydia listened as Tim went on to tell a story about a swash buckling, four eyed pirate who had retired from sailing the seven seas, buried his treasure out on the island, (pointing at the island that they could see halfway across the lake) and settled down to a life of leisure, living in the Birch Cabin. He went on with a hollow voice, "One stormy night, a gypsy who had been double crossed by the pirate, back in his pirating days, crept up and threw a black cat onto the roof of the cabin." "It was the bonniest little cat you ever did see!" interjected Emily cheerily. Tim, paying no heed to this interruption, went on in a whisper, "The pirate heard a scratching noise and came out to investigate just as the full moon was emerging from a break in the storm clouds. He looked up and saw the cat, silouetted against the moon and he was so frightened, he died of a heart attack on the spot. Now he haunts the cabin unless..." "Unless you rub the head of the four eyed pirate, on the door of that shed over there, three time before you go to bed at night," finished Emily. "You guys are just teasing me," said Lydia with a searching look.

Emily changed the subject, "Look! There's a robin. Let's throw this worm over there." Emily was never disturbed by all the eating and being eaten that goes on in nature, not even as a child. Her little friend had a less pragmatic view of the situation however and they ended up tucking the worm safely under a rock.

"Do you remember Farkus?" asked Tim as he watched Lydia wander back to where her parents were sitting nearby. "That wasn't his real name," answered Emily. "No, but he's the one that told us the pirate story, holding a flashlight up to his face for dramatic effect and all, remember? We pretended that we were really scared," said Tim. "I remember you wished there really was a treasure out on that island. You looked longingly out there the rest of that week," said Emily.

Farkus, that was the only name anyone could remember calling him, was a year older than Tim. He had stayed in Cabin 2

(Birch) the first year the Vincys stayed in Cabin 1 (Spruce). Farkus was a bully in school, at least that is what he had told everyone. But he usually took a vacation from bullying when he was at the lake. Instead of intimidation, he tried to impress Tim and the Brooke girls with his vast store of knowledge and daring antics. They were amused by his various machinations.

He showed them how to place a penny on the railroad tracks and then come back the next day to collect their flattened copper souvenir. Emily still had one she used as a bookmark, but don't try it nowadays, you'll get a fine for trespassing.

Farkus would sneak firecrackers from his older brother's stash. He would light them and then throw them into the pond, so they would ignite underwater, until a short fuse ended that fun. The next day, with a bandaged hand and a determination to make up for the previous day's miscalculation, he dressed up like an old lady with clothes and a gray wig from the playhouse. A maroon shawl, glasses, and long stockings were added to complete the disguise. He took Tim and the girls up to the road and had them hide in the bushes, to watch, as he lay down alongside the road in the tall grass. A car drove by and kept going. Old lady Farkus slid over a bit closer to the road. A second car was coming down the road, it slowed, then, came to a screeching stop and a man and women ran out of the car. Farkus got scared and rolled onto his stomach crying. The couple couldn't see his face and by the time the man had gently rolled him over to see what was wrong, the woman had already called an ambulance. That was a Friday. They never saw Farkus again.

Emily's attention had turned toward a small rowboat that was sitting idly on the beach, promising adventure to anyone daring enough to cast off.

Tim noticed a certain gleam in her eye and the peculiar way her lips curled at the end of her smile. He loved that look. He knew what she was thinking. "I'll get some oars!" he said, and was gone before she could answer. She had wrestled the boat into the lake by the time he returned empty handed. "The oars were in the boat," she said as she waited impatiently for Tim to help her climb in. "I'll row first," she said after getting settled.

"Take her out to sea Emily, let's stretch her legs!" said Tim expansively from the back, bench seat.

It was true. Tim had looked longingly at the island that Farkus summer, dreaming of buried treasure. The following summer, Tim returned, equipped with a White's Coinmaster metal detector that he had gotten for his eleventh birthday. He and Emily scoured the island and unearthed 56 cents in small change, a mercury dime, and a sterling silver ring that had the word: "Peace" engraved on it.

As they rowed out from shore, they were observed by Mr. Brooke from the dock at Cabin 3. Harold had worked in an iron foundry since he was 18. At work he wore steel toed, leather boots that had elastic in the sides to keep them on, instead of laces, so they could be kicked off quickly if molten iron spilled into them. At the lake he went bare foot or wore sandals.

In the foundry, he breathed core gas and dust. At the resort he enjoyed fresh air and the smell of the white pines that towered over the property and gave it a timeless feel. In the summer, there was no escape from the heat of the electric induction furnace during the workday. No escape except to the lake for a week of vacation.

He took a great deal of pride in his work. Lorraine and the girls adored him. They fussed over him when he came home from work and he let them.

Harold was getting ready to fish for bluegills from his dock. He preferred fishing with a bobber and live bait so he could just sit and relax, enjoying the day. He assumed that the fish would either find his bait eventually, or, if they were aware of his bait, that they would get hungry eventually. Either way, he would wait them out. After all, he was on vacation.

William Vincy, a salesman from Belvidere, Illinois, smoked Camel straights, drank his coffee strong and black, and called a shot of brandy "medcine." He scoffed at the idea of *diet* soda or *light* beer and put high octane gas in his Cadillac. He wanted everyone to know he had money, but he was tighter than bark on a tree when it came to spending it. He arrived at the

Hideaway, for the first time, in August of 1994 and brought his wife Clare and their only child, Timothy, along with him.

Tim and Emily met that summer. Emily lamented that the street address of the resort had been changed from Hydro Lane to a bunch of numbers. "Names are charming but numbers are just cold and sterile," she had said with a cross look on her 7 year old face. Tim never forgot that for some reason.

Tim had told a scary campfire story, about a cave filled with rats, and Emily never forgot that either. Rats were ok out in the open, but in a confined space? That was just creepy. The two became inseparable friends.

William didn't come to the Hideaway to relax like Harold, he didn't even know what relaxation was. He came to west central Wisconsin to pursue sales leads. He liked the idea of being able to say on the phone, "I'm staying at the lake next week; I'll stop by with some samples." Bill Vincy had as much passion for sales as he did for vices and soon had many accounts in the area so that in 1998 he moved his family to Minneapolis, Minnesota but continued to return to the lake every year like the Brookes.

Bill and his son Tim spent a great deal of time together despite Bill's being often on the road. He encouraged him in his education, attended his activities when he could, took him fishing and to the races, and even bought him a car when he was 16, a 1970 Chevelle. Bill and Tim spent many hours working on that car together.

Bill was fishing from his dock at the Spruce Cabin. His method of fishing was a frenzied application of his occupational training. He preferred to cast a spinner bait and retrieve it fast enough to keep the spinner blade churning on top of the water. If that did not work, he would select a different color or style and try that, convinced that the smallmouth bass and northern pike were out there, and would strike if he could just present them with an enticing product.

As he fished, he was also a witness to the slow progress being made by Emily as she worked the oars. He admired her and hoped that she would bear his grandchildren someday. He had even told Tim as much 2 years ago; "Why don't you put a ring on that little gal's finger and knock out a few grandkids for me to spoil?" Tim *had* tried to put a ring on her finger 2 years ago. It happened in the very spot that they were now heading to.

In 2002, when Tim and Elizabeth were both 17, they were considered to be "going together." What that phrase means to you, the reader of this story, I'm not exactly sure but certainly they did things that "going together" couples do. They held hands at the campfires, went for walks, spent time together, (although Tim still spent more time with Emily) and went to one or two movies. It was nothing too serious. It is not clear whether or not they even exchanged a kiss for neither one would ever say. The following year they "broke up" by mutual consent and remained friends.

The year after that, when Tim was 19, he flirted with Tricia. Still, he spent most of his time with the infinitely patient Emily.

Finally, in 2005, when Tim was 20 and Emily 18, a romantic element began to creep into their friendship. It grew the following year and in 2007 they exchanged their first kiss. In 2008, Tim had tried to expand upon the passion and duration of that first kiss to a point that exceeded Emily's idea of propriety and she had awkwardly separated herself from him. She spent the rest of that week in the arduous task of rebuilding his self-esteem.

On a Friday in August of 2009, after spending the week with Emily as always, Tim had decided that she was the object of his desires. He had come to the conclusion that she could make him happy for the rest of his life, so, out on the island, on a little clearing that opened to a five mile view to the north, and with big white clouds floating overhead like in a dream, Tim, slipping a ring on her finger, (a sterling silver ring that had the word 'peace' engraved on it) said the words that Emily had dreamed of hearing from him since she was a young girl; "Emily Brooke, I love you, will you marry me?"

Emily was not surprised to hear these words and she had her answer prepared, but when she saw the ring, she was stunned. She had no idea that he still had that silver ring that they had found together. It was only five dollars worth of silver and an iconic phrase from the 1960's, but it was the perfect symbol of their friendship. It was more valuable to her than any diamond ring could ever be.

Memory after memory rushed to her consciousness without regard for her sanity. For the first time in her life she seemed to have no control over her facial expressions and was dimly aware of a tear running down her cheek. It was as if she were inside her body somewhere, a mere spectator to what her outer body was doing. She felt suddenly small, like a pinpoint in an infinite cascade of universes. Her world was suddenly spinning around in slow motion as if she were a single iron filing in a whirlpool of magnetic flux. Time seemed to slow to a crawl while she was being sucked into a black hole, impotent against the bone crushing force of its gravitational pull. Sounds came to her ear as if she were underwater.

Tim, not surprised that his declaration and proposal had left her speechless, waited patiently for her to regain her composure. He was oblivious to the cosmic drama that was rending her.

Emily sank down into the tall grass and the closer contact with the earth gradually affected her. Her breathing slowed and her heartbeat resumed its normal pulse. Color came back into her face. Objects came back into focus. Gradually, she regained control of her movement and reaching for Tim's hand, placed the ring into it, folded his fingers over it, and still holding his hand in hers, said with sympathetic decisiveness; "Perhaps... someday."

Chapter 3   Sunday Continued

The next day after Tim's proposal was Saturday and the Brookes were driving back home. Elizabeth, 8 months pregnant, and Jim, her husband had stayed in the Cedar Cabin for the week. They lived only 6 blocks away from the Brooke residence in Milwaukee but drove separately.

The stress of the previous day had left Emily feeling physically ill. The ever-attentive ears of Lorraine, in the front seat, heard a quiet sniffle in the back, despite Harold's fumbling with the radio. She handed Emily a Kleenex.

Emily felt like a tissue, a used one that had been tossed out a car window on a rainy night, into the gutter of a street that had once been known as Pleasant Avenue but was now five thousand nine hundred sixty seventh and a half street. Tissue Emily had then been run over by a Ford Pinto, and washed into the storm sewer where she was chewed to bits by a rat. The bits of Emily were flushed along until she was dumped into the river where she sank into the muck at the bottom. The muck was contaminated with toxic waste from a factory upstream that made fly swatters and toilet plungers.

That was how Emily was feeling as Harold searched the a.m. stations for a talk show that might be talkin' Packers. Harold stopped when he heard a bluegrass song that was apparently familiar to him. Emily was vaguely aware that he had mumbled something about a genuine Kentucky coal miner's daughter. Her ears picked up on the lyrics: "Where the sun comes up, about 10 in the morning and the sun goes down, about 3 in the day, and you fill your cup, with whatever bitter brew you're drinkin' and you spend your life, digging coal, from the bottom of your grave. . ." [1]

All Emily's future prospects seemed to her young mind to be summed up in those lyrics. She imagined that her fate was a life of broken-hearted loneliness, living alone with just a cat to console her and she didn't even like cats much. Later, she would look back at that time in her life with some embarrassment, but at the time, the pain was real.

When the song was over, a tear was streaming down the cheek of Emily. The ever-attentive eye of Lorraine saw the tear, even though she was in the front seat helping Harold drive. She turned off the radio which got the attention of Harold. Lorraine cast a knowing glance toward the back seat and Harold understood. Tricia also noticed and slid over in the back seat next to her sister and held her hand. Emily laid her head on Tricia's shoulder and sobbed heavily as the Bonneville rolled past the dashed white lines that seemed to endlessly stitch the two lanes of asphalt together that formed southbound Interstate 94.

The Brooke family shared in each other's joys and sorrows. This practice made the joys more enjoyable and the sorrows more bearable. Emily's healing had begun on that ride home and about a month later she was able to write Tim a letter. Tim had brought that very letter with him, to the Hideaway, two years later, and some others that he had received from her. In fact, he had that first letter in his pocket as they rowed out to the island.

I have obtained the original copies of those letters from the owner of the resort. He found them in the nightstand drawer

---

[1] Patty Loveless, Mountain Soul, 2001

after Tim checked out of the cabin. Here is what that first letter said:

September 25, 2009

Dear Timothy,
I hope this letter finds you in good health. I was rather ill for a while but am feeling better now. We are all very excited here because Beth gave birth to a healthy, 8 pound baby girl on the 18ᵗʰ. She and Jim are very proud. They named her Liz, can you imagine!? (Trish has been unbearable.) My class load is light so I'm working more hours at the nursing home. I've also had more time to think about some of the things you talked about at the lake. Your philosophical position confuses me. It seems riddled with contradiction. You've changed in some subtle way that I don't understand. I was caught off guard, and didn't know how to respond to some of the things you were saying.
Now that I have had time to organize my thoughts, I will attempt to explain to you what I believe. I believe in infinite existence, and everything that exists, exists in relation to an 'other.' We relate through the faculties of the soul: intellect and will. The ultimate reality for me is mind or idea. The physical world is the result of a soul experiencing time, that is, having the ability to choose. I agree, this world is real enough while we are in it, but it is illusory in the sense that it is transient.
If all that truly exists is matter and energy, and our life is no more than the result of physical processes and blind purposeless forces, if free will is an illusion, as you say, than how can I understand what you mean when you say that you love me?
I understand love to be an act of the will, a free will. Willing the good of another, for their own sake, and then sharing in their joy, has infinite potential. Relationships formed with sole regard to the potential benefit to self are finite and ultimately make an object of the other, which leads to isolation and loneliness. If your love is not rooted in the will, than I fear it is nothing more than emotion and

25

feeling. Electrical impulses and chemical reactions are not a solid foundation to build a relationship on.
Do write to me Timothy, please, I have been miserably vexed since we last parted.

Affectionately Yours,
 Emily

They pulled the boat up on the sandy beach on the south end of the island and explored for a while like old times. Eventually, they found their way to the clearing where the ill-fated proposal had taken place. They sat, enjoying the view, for a few minutes, without saying a word. Then, producing the letter from his pocket, and looking at Emily, he asked, "Does my being physically attracted to you disqualify me? I mean, I am you know, attracted to you." Color rose in Emily's cheeks as she glanced from the letter to Tim's earnest face. She answered, "And I, you." After a brief pause, she continued, "No, but there needs to be more than attraction."

They sat again in silence until a warm summer breeze rustled Emily's hair and roused Tim's attention. "It looks pretty dark to the west. We should head back," he observed. They returned without incident. The dark cloud blew over and the sky was clear again as they pulled the boat up on shore. Tim and Emily parted company but not without her having secured a commitment from him to play Aggravation later that evening.

Emily ran into Elizabeth on the way back to her cabin. "Tim and I are playing Aggravation later, are you in?" "Maybe," she answered. "How are things going between you two?" Emily's face brightened but she answered evasively, "Fine. Where's Liz Marie?" "She's taking a nap with Jim so I have time to talk. I saw you two rowing back from the island." They sat down at a picnic table and Lorraine came out of the cabin carrying a plastic pitcher and joined them. "Would you girls like some lemonade?" "Sure, thanks," answered Elizabeth and glancing at Emily's hand. "I thought maybe I'd see a ring on your finger when you got back." "Oh don't pester the poor girl. It'll happen in due time if

26

it's meant to be," remonstrated Lorraine. "Mom, you and dad lived in the same neighborhood, you could keep an eye on things, I mean, it was a different situation." Then, turning to Emily, she continued, "Em, I just want to say that I think you made the right decision two years ago. I think he was still unsettled from all that he had gone through with, well, you know. But I sense a change in him and I think he came here this week for you." Emily dropped her head slightly at these words and her eyes were cast down in deep thought.

Tricia came out of the cabin wearing a pair of cheap, pink sunglasses. "Did you steal those from the playhouse?" questioned Elizabeth. "No, I'm just borrowing them," answered Tricia with sassy innocence. Then she playfully stuck her tongue out at her sister. This exchange roused Emily. "I think they add an aura of mystery to your look." "I know," agreed Tricia simply as she stood with one hand on her hip. Her other hand was occupied with twirling her long hair around her finger. "Beth was just urging me to throw myself at Tim and beg him to marry me. I suppose you agree with her," said Emily. "I was doing no such thing," countered Elizabeth, "I just don't think that you have to agree on everything before you get engaged. If he's ready to settle down and start a family, and if you think he would be a good father and husband, then marry him. You'll have the rest of your life to discuss philosophy or whatever." Tricia took off her shades and sat down with a more serious demeanor. "I would have married him two years ago, but I understand why *you* didn't. I agree with Liz, he's a catch and some girl's gonna snap him up before long. Get that ring back and then you can work things out later."

Harold came out of the cabin and saw the estrogen council that was taking place at the picnic table. He turned on his heel and went back into the cabin. "I think Tim is going to turn out to be a lot more like your father than his own father," observed Lorraine to Emily. "Harold used to poke around on cars, and," Lorraine paused and leaned in toward the center of the group, drawing her daughters into the secret circle of her confidence, "and, when we were young, he could not keep his

27

hands off me," "Mother!" exclaimed Elizabeth. Tricia and Emily were looking at each other and smiling, "but when you girls came along," Lorraine continued, "he always provided for us."

Emily appreciated all the advice, she really did, but she was operating on a different plane from the other Brooke females. After a while, she went inside with the others to get dinner ready. While they bustled around, she was thinking to herself about Tim's parents. One of Emily's all time favorite books was, "The House Of Mirth" by Edith Wharton. Tim's mother, Clare, reminded Emily of Miss Lily Bart. Clare and Lily had both died in the same tragic manner. Tim had been the one who had discovered her still, lifeless body one year to the day, after the divorce.

William Vincy was a born salesman. He could sell a ketchup popsicle to a woman in a white dress. Bill sold carpet for a large flooring distributor. He made sales calls on retailers that sold flooring, some of which were managed by women. In June of 2008, he was entertaining a client, one thing led to another, and the another crossed the boundary of marital fidelity. The incident was the nail in the coffin of an already dying relationship.

Clare had been a nurturing mother when Tim was young. She was more or less content with an infant, then toddler and finally preschooler to distract her from that creeping emptiness, that ennui that her set often experience. But as she grew older, and Tim entered school, physiological changes began to take place. Clare was diagnosed with clinical depression and prescribed various medications with disagreeable side effects. There were days when she could not summon the strength to crawl out of bed and dress and there were nights when she would lay awake for hours, desperate for relief from her fatigue.

Clare had been raised to exist in a class of society that required substantial capital to sustain. Bill spent long hours on the road, earning his commission, in order that he might maintain the lifestyle that she was accustomed to. A big house filled with nice things, a new car, and a credit card with an obscenely high limit, only served to form a thin veneer to obscure her horrid loneliness.

The path of a peace filled soul lies along the fine line that separates chaos and boredom. Humanity requires a certain amount of stress in order to thrive, but the key is in the balance. How many of us oscillate back and forth between one extreme and the other? Neither Bill nor Clare could find that balance. Bill's life had become a frenzied pursuit of money. He insulated himself from the stress of this fast paced lifestyle with his vices. Clare was surrounded by all the material that Bill's money could buy and was left with utterly no purpose. Relief from her tedium came in the form of a little, chalky white pill. Their relationship withered and died like a plant left in a dark closet with no sunlight and no one to water it.

After the divorce, Tim lived with his mother, but would often stay with his father for a few days at a time. Returning home after one such visit, Tim noticed signs about the house that indicated that something was wrong. These and perhaps an underlying sense of inevitability prepared him somewhat for the ghastly discovery of his dead mother. She was lying on the floor next to her bed. A trickle of blood from her mouth had dried to a dark brownish color and sharply contrasted the ghost white color of her face. She had been dead for two days by the time he found her and her body exhibited an eerie, rigid stillness. With this image fresh in his mind, Tim remembered thinking it odd that the 911 operator had asked if he had checked her pulse and if he was sure that she was dead. He remembered also, how the flashing, blue, emergency vehicle light, filtered through the window and alternately illuminated and darkened the picture of his grandfather, which hung on the wall of the living room, where he waited for the coroner to finish her work.

Later that evening, that curious board, punched full of holes that were sized just right for colorful marbles to nestle into, was set up and the Aggravation commenced. Tim and Emily were joined by Elizabeth, Jim, and Harold, while Lorraine entertained Liz.

"Where's Trish?" inquired Emily as she rolled a six. "She's meeting a friend at The View for a drink," responded Harold. "Roll again," Elizabeth reminded Emily. "What friend?" asked Emily. "Oh, I think her name is Tiffany. They were friends in school but she moved up to this area about a year ago," answered Harold as he shook a 4 and advanced his marble to the center of the board. "I'm concerned about her drinking. Sometimes, she doesn't know when to quit. She's vulnerable like that," said Emily with an imploring look that seemed to ask if anyone agreed with her assessment of her sister's situation. "Have you talked to her about your concern?" questioned Jim. Elizabeth knocked Harold out of the center. "Sorry, you probably would have been stuck there a long time anyway," she offered as consolation. "What comes around goes around." Harold said that at least once every time they played. Emily answered Jim's question; "I have. She just said that she had not had a drink in two weeks, which was probably true. It's when she does drink though... she just seems so restless lately." "She's always been restless," observed Elizabeth. "Maybe we should go over there later," suggested Tim. He had not rolled a one or a six yet. All his marbles were still stuck in base. "Maybe you should check your dice and make sure there's a six on it," advised Harold. Harold and Elizabeth were very competitive when it came to games, which is strange, at least in the case of Elizabeth who was generally reserved and serious. "It's Sunday. I wouldn't think she'd find much going on over there to get caught up in on a Sunday," pointed out Jim hopefully. Jim was a likeable enough guy, steady, reliable, trustworthy and honest, much like his spouse Elizabeth. "Is she still thinking about studying cinematography?" inquired Tim. "She's starting this fall actually, it's your turn Emily," answered Harold. "That's great. She'll have something to focus her considerable energy on," said Tim. He finally rolled a one and got a marble out on to the board. Jim shook next and rolled a four. He examined his options and realized he had only one possible move. He sheepishly knocked Tim's marble out, saying, "I didn't have any choice, sorry bud." "I guess that's why it's called Aggravation," said Elizabeth. "At least

30

you got out for one roll, honey," said Emily with playful optimism, rubbing Tim's back as if to cheer him and making an exaggeratedly hopeful face.

Aggravation is a game that requires little thought and, consequently, lends itself well as a background to conversation, adding the amusement that the unpredictable results of a chance roll of the dice provides and affording well acquainted players the opportunity to give each other a hard time and not so well acquainted players, the opportunity to become better acquainted.

"Why don't you ask your *honey* if he would like some of that nasty stuff you have cooked up on the stove?" asked Elizabeth. Emily, who usually measured her words carefully, had just sort of let the "honey" slip out without intending to say it, although, she did not regret it either. Elizabeth was not the only one who caught it. Tim sat musing about the implications the term of endearment might have while Emily turned to him and asked politely, "Would you care for a cup of stinging nettle tea?" "I would love to sample a cup, thank you," replied Tim diplomatically. While Emily, with a curt smile and slight nod of the head to rebuff her sister, went for the tea, Harold offered to trade dice with Tim. Everyone else had at least one marble home and Tim's were all still in his base. "No thanks. I think this dice is going to heat up anytime now," said Tim confidently. The funny part was, he ended up winning.

Emily returned with a steamy mug of green liquid and handed it to Tim with some encouragement, "It's very high in vitamin A." "Vitamin A, the very thing I need after a day of adventure at the old Hideaway. Has anyone met the couple staying in Spruce?" inquired Tim. No one had.

Emily had gone into the bedroom to fetch a light sweater. It was dusk, and a cool, but welcome breeze was coming in through the lakeside windows. As she closed her dresser drawer, something outside the window caught her eye. A white, nightgown shaped apparition, was gliding down the road toward the shed. "Oh, the poor dear," said Emily to herself. She returned to the kitchen and signaled Tim to follow her outside, a

31

development that was not even commented on by the others for there was nothing remarkable about the two of them wandering off at odd times with some sort of scheme at hand. "Look," said Emily when they got outside, pointing in the direction of the little ghost. They followed, keeping out of sight, until the white figure reached the door of the shed. There it paused, a white arm reached up and made a rubbing motion, and then floated back toward the Birch Cabin. "I should go to her," suggested Emily. "No," urged Tim, "it's part of the experience." Emily reflected on having done the same thing as a young girl, and seemingly none the worse for it, agreed with a nod, "Quite so."

After their return to the cabin, other games were played until Tricia got back at about 11:00. "You're home early," observed Elizabeth. "I couldn't find much trouble to get into on a Sunday night I guess. Anyway, I met the couple from the Spruce Cabin. They're a hoot. What are you drinking Tim?" responded Tricia. Tim had asked for a second cup of nettle tea but had only finished half of it. "It's stinging nettle tea," answered Emily for Tim, her eyes all a shimmer with pride. "Oh, I thought it was lime vodka sour," said Tricia with disappointment. "Well, I'm tired. See you all in the morning."

Tricia was home safe and off to bed and everyone seemed a bit relieved and suddenly tired themselves. The party broke up and everyone turned in for the night.

Chapter 4 Monday

Emily was sitting in the sand of the seldom-used volleyball court with her niece Liz Marie. (Emily always added her middle name.) They had found a tiny, blackish gray snapping turtle. Its shell was only about one inch in diameter. It had crawled out of the sand and they were waiting to see if any more would crawl out from the same hole.

Every June, snapping turtles would dig down into the sand with their back legs and then deposit up to two dozen, ping pong ball sized eggs about a foot under ground. The eggs would hatch in mid August to early September.

Tim soon joined them and then Lydia. They built an elaborate sand castle for the lone snapper while they were waiting. Tim always liked to watch Emily as she interacted with children. She was more or less a big child herself, childlike, not childish. Children could sense that she genuinely liked to be spending time with them and they enjoyed her presence. She had mastered different techniques for correcting errant behavior without getting stressed out. As Tim watched, he realized all three sisters had this same ability. It seemed to come natural to them and so, he reasoned, they must have learned it from their mother. That was true.

Elizabeth came over and took Liz to the dress up house.

Tim stood up and was looking in that direction when he noticed Emily look up and past him with a smile. He guessed that someone was approaching from behind him but before he could turn he heard; "Greetings, fellow omnivores!" This odd salutation had somehow found its way out from behind a tangle of long gray beard which was worn by a slight figured, bright eyed, old scutter named Benteen Willis. His greeting was odd, his countenance was odd, his name was odd, but the oddest thing about old Benteen was his diet. He was whittling on a fuzzy stick that appeared to be sumac. "Are you digging for turtle eggs?" said Benteen.

When he got down to the pliable new growth at the center of his stick, he popped it in his mouth. In her excitement, Emily uncharacteristically ignored his question and asked one of her own. "Did you just eat sumac?"

One summer, when she was a teenager, she had brought a copy of "Stalking The Wild Asparagus" along with her. She and Tim had gone on foraging adventures together. They had even lived off the "fat of the lan'" for a day.

Benteen was deeply impressed that she had identified the sumac from just a twig. He responded enthusiastically, "Sure, I've been eating all morning. There's more food around here than you can shake a stick at. A sumac stick even." He coughed a little

34

laugh into his hand at his own joke. "Been eatin' lambs quarter, milkweed, wood sorrel, got some stinging nettles and Solomon seal roots in the cabin I'm gonna cook up later, maybe some puffballs too. I've never eaten snapping turtle eggs did you?" Before Emily could answer he continued, "Now I have eaten snapping turtle. Makes the best soup you ever did taste guaranteed." Emily and Tim were intrigued. Lydia was turning green. Benteen went on in his shrill, sing song voice about his hillbilly ways and all the various plants he had eaten. Suddenly he stopped in mid sentence and asked, "Would you all like to go foraging?"

Spontaneity was one trait that Tim and Emily had in common. They said good bye to Lydia, left the snapping turtle to guard his castle as best he might, and followed Benteen Willis as he rambled on about eating acorns, maple seeds, hazelnuts, elderberries, bull thistle, burdock...

Benteen's mother died when he was young. He grew up in cities with his father who was a con artist by trade. Benteen was a quick study and the transient lifestyle suited him so he followed in his father's footsteps.

When he was in his late twenties, Benteen was making his living dealing Three-Card Monte, in Cleveland, Ohio, until a mark got wise, a big burly man with no sense of humor, and pummeled him. The shill he worked with got scared and ran away with all the money leaving poor Benteen with nothing but bruises and the blood soaked shirt on his back.

In this vulnerable state, he was discovered by a good Samaritan who happened to belong to a religious sect that preached with absolute certainty that the world was going to end on August 8, 1972.

This group was recruiting people from all walks of life, and encouraging them to sell all of their belongings, to help finance a settlement in Nevada, where they would ride out the calamitous day of doom and then repopulate the earth after the flood of destruction had subsided.

Benteen had nothing to sell but he had a valuable skill to offer and he signed on with the group, which called themselves,

"The Sons And Daughters of the Never Ending World Settlement" or SAD NEWS. Anyway, Benteen joined the sect, with the same self-interest that had motivated him to throw in with others that had a good hustle going.

Two things happened while Benteen was involved with SAD NEWS. He met Margaret and he became alarmed at all the possible scenarios that could actually lead to the end of the world, as we know it. He had no regard for the August 8, 1972 date, thought the leaders of the group would be long gone, by that time, with a good chunk of the money, but he didn't care. He had food, shelter, and relative safety, more than he had had at any other time in his life. The threat of economic collapse, nuclear war, or natural disaster, weighed heavily on his mind however, because for the first time in his life, he had something, or rather, someone, to live for.

Well, August 8, 1972, came and went and it turns out the leadership of SAD NEWS really believed their doctrines. They were genuinely astonished when, on August 9, 1972, time clocks were still being punched, trucks were making their deliveries, schools were admitting students for their indoctrination, stores were serving customers and all was business as usual. Instead of being thankful that the day of reckoning had passed them by, they reviewed their data, made some adjustments, and calculated a new date; September 1, 1979.

At this point, most of their following drifted away, including Benteen and Margaret, who married and moved into a trailer court on the outskirts of Cleveland.

Benteen earned money by picking up any scrap metal that people wanted hauled away and selling it to scrap yards. He drove an old Chevy Stepside, (three speed on the column, 292 straight six, wooden bed) and Margaret rode shotgun.

He soon took a liking to the variety and form of the junk he was hauling so he learned how to solder, braze, and weld and endeavored to fabricate and sell scrap metal art. He sold the spoon and fork crab, the rebar and rusty pipe cowboy with genuine spur gear spurs and cap gun six-shooter. He sold candleholders, plant stands and garden ornamentation. He made

36

wine racks, coffee tables and picture frames. Benteen could make anything his imagination and inspiration could conjure up. Meanwhile, Margaret took to repurposing old furniture. She also dabbled in painting, wood carving, and wood burning on old weathered barn boards and driftwood. Most of this craftwork was done in a garage owned by Margaret's mother.

They traveled to flea markets and craft shows, selling their creations, which, along with a few side jobs here and there, kept them afloat financially for a few years until Margaret's mother died. When the estate was settled, Margaret inherited $68,000.

They decided to move "up north" and bought some land about thirty miles outside Madison, Wisconsin, where they built a very modest cabin and lived off the grid like homesteaders.

Eventually, they moved an old shed onto the property out by the road (their cabin was not visible from the road) and with the last of their inheritance money, paid the power company to set a pole and install a transformer so they could have electricity in the shed. The shed served two purposes: it was the studio for the creation of their eclectic art and the storefront for marketing it.

As the years went by, their fame spread as buyers who had money, and liked to buy odd things from odd people, came around and then told friends about the charming couple that made art in the old shed outside town.

These were peaceful years, but Benteen and Margaret were getting restless. Eventually, they decided to hire someone to run the store and spent three or four months a year traveling about the Midwest, collecting material and inspiration.

When Tim and Emily returned, Lydia was wearing a fancy little ballroom dress with white lace on the sleeves, a blue scarf, and a sunbonnet. She was having a tea party with Tricia who was decked out in a fur coat, pink sunglasses, and a fireman's hat. Lydia's mom was talking with Elizabeth while she pushed Liz in a swing. Liz was wearing a princess outfit complete with crown and glass slippers.

Emily joined the tea party and Tim walked over to the swing set. He pretended not to notice Liz swinging there and when she brushed up against him, he fell to the ground in a most dramatic fashion. Then he got up scratching his head in utter confusion as to what unseen force could have blindsided him. He managed to position himself in such a way that when Liz swung out again, her feet just touched his back. This light touch sent him somersaulting across the ground. This was positively the most hilarious thing Liz had ever witnessed in all her 23 months of life and it was every bit as funny the fourth time as it was the first. The women were all smiling sweet smiles that only a child's laughter could produce.

Lizzy's reaction seems to be the universal reaction to antics of the sort that Tim had engaged in. If you don't believe me, try it for yourself.

Eventually, Tim was played out. Entertaining children can be exhausting, even for a healthy, athletic, 26 year old. I guess everything worthwhile, even a child's laughter, requires some effort.

Meanwhile, the tea party was going along famously. Lydia had told the older girls about all the boys who had chased her at school. Emily had told about a boy who had chased her and Tricia was now telling about all the boys that she had chased. That was a familiar subject to Emily so her attention drifted to the conversation between Tim, Elizabeth, and Lydia's mom. They were talking about which cabins they liked best, plans for next summer, and then something about the lake being a great place for kids to spend a week each summer. Emily distinctly heard Tim say, "Yes I know, I would like to bring my own kids here someday." Emily shuddered so hard that she spilled her muddy water tea. With round eyes, she cast a cautious glance in their direction to convince herself that it was really Tim who had said it. She turned back, thoughtfully, color rising in her cheeks, and a barely discernible smile forming on her lips, and pretended to sip her tea. None of these proceedings were lost on Tricia who was studying her sister attentively from behind her pink shades.

Emily had never heard Tim speak of having children before. Two years ago, all he had talked about was how much money he was going to make at his new job and what he was going to spend it on. He also spoke about college and some of the ideas he had soaked up in that institution of higher learning. He had seemed firmly rooted in materialism then. Talk of children was further evidence of a change that Emily discerned in Tim.

Eventually, the tea party broke up. Lydia wanted to go swimming. Emily found a quiet spot to do some reading. Tim had been invited to dine with the Brookes later so he went to take a shower and maybe a nap in the hammock he had set up that morning.

After dinner, wine was poured, beers were opened, and the conversation turned to reminiscing about past summers at the resort.

Tricia had been waiting for an opportune time to stir things up a bit. After all, it was in her nature to do so. Looking at Tim she asked, "Do you remember that summer when you were flirting with me, and Emily got so jealous," "I did not!" interrupted Emily. "So jealous, that she spent half the week reading your car magazines so she could impress you with her knowledge of crankshafts or whatever? Well a few months after you and Emily, ah, last saw each other, that was what, two years now? A few months after anyway, Emily was still moping around so I talked her into going on a double date with me. It was a disaster mostly, but one funny thing happened."

In 2004, Emily had spent a good deal of time pouring over Tim's Hot Rod, Car Craft, and Super Stock and Drag Illustrated magazines. She was a voracious reader. Although classic literature was her reading of choice, she found the magazines amusing. It was like learning a new language. She read product reviews and how to articles. She learned about all the latest engine build-ups and performance enhancements and she smirked at all the scantily clad women depicted. (The juxtaposition of the last two phrases was pure coincidence.)

Emily wondered why those women would degrade themselves in such a way.

Tricia had scandalized both Emily and Elizabeth by casually mentioning that she would pose in a bikini if she could be pictured with an aqua green 55 Chevy. That was her favorite color because it complimented her green eyes and strawberry blonde hair. If you are wondering about the probability of that scenario, listen, Tricia Brooke would have rocked the cover of Hot Rod. The editors could have had her standing next to a Ford Pinto. It wouldn't have mattered. No one would have noticed the car anyway. I'll just leave it at that.

The internal combustion engine became a sort of hobby for Emily, although she had never touched a wrench other than to hand it to someone. She still picked up car magazines from time to time. It was a nice change of pace from the complex sentence structure of the books she usually read. Plus, she was able to have intelligent mechanical conversations with Harold and Tim.

Elizabeth and Jim joined the table as Tricia continued, "I set Em up with a fella named Monte, a friend of a friend sort of thing. He was into cars so I thought it might be a good match." Emily was rolling her eyes. The Brookes had already heard this story so Tricia was mostly looking at Tim while she talked. He was beaming. "We went out to eat. He turned out to be all talk. He was driving us all crazy with his nonstop bragging. It seems that Monte had done just about everything there was to do in this world, and done it faster and better than anyone else ever had. Emily was being a saint, of course, until he got around to the subject of cars."

Tricia's audience evidenced a heightened degree of attention at this point. Emily sat with her arms crossed but an adorable smirk on her face. She was pretending to be embarrassed but was secretly glad that Tim was hearing about the date. "Well, he started talking about how fast his car was and how many races he had won and all that. Then our Em starts asking him questions. You can imagine the questions she could ask right? And old Monte, he just stood there with his mouth open while she smacked him around with car talk. He didn't say hardly a word the rest of the night."

Emily had dressed with extra concern for modesty the night of the date and she had felt compelled to speak with even more eloquent proper English as a counterweight to the slang and occasional expletive that spilled out of Monte's mouth. Her conservative, feminine, appearance and speech seemed to encourage Monte. He assumed her to be naïve and impressionable.

Leaning forward slightly for emphasis, he had told Emily that his car had a 350 four barrel and that it was "bored" out. He then leaned back, confident that this information was sure to melt Emily into a puddle of admiration.

Emily, exasperated with Monte's ignorant bravado, began an inquisition; "Really? Does the four barrel have mechanical or vacuum actuated secondaries?" Monte replied, "agh..." She continued, "Boring the cylinders of your 350 probably added, what, 5 cubic inches, and not much horsepower? What performance modifications have you made? Did you raise the compression ratio? Did you have the manifolds port matched? What's your cam lift and duration?" Monte was reduced to a series of er's and um's while the interrogation continued, "What's the rear differential gear ratio? Is it open or limited slip? Ever consider a multiple spark discharge ignition or a high stall torque converter?" For the first time that night, Monte was at a loss for words. Emily finished him off with, "It sounds like you might as well just install a nitrous set up."

About three weeks after that, Emily had been asked out on a date by Walter, who was in her English Literature class. He was into books so she thought it might be a good match. He suggested a very fine restaurant and she accepted.

Tricia had helped Emily pick out a new formal dress for the occasion and then Tricia helped her with her hair. It was done up in an elegant twisted chignon revealing her slim neck and diamond earrings that she had borrowed from her mother. "You look stunning!" gushed Tricia when they were done.

"Really? Maybe I should wear something else," faltered Emily, disconcerted at the compliment. "Just relax. You've been studying and working so hard you deserve a little fun. Listen, if you're having a good time at dinner, slip your shoe off and rub his leg with your foot. Then ask him to take you dancing. There's a live band playing at the Meet Market tonight."

The Meet Market was a popular club in Milwaukee where Tricia worked part time. "If dinner is a bust, just tell him you have a headache and come home early." Emily was giving her sister the crinkled nose look. "I'll be keeping my shoes on, thank you, and I thought I might suggest coffee at the Brewhouse. They have poetry reading tonight." "You hate poetry!" objected Tricia. "I don't hate it. I just don't appreciate it. But Walter does. I saw him reading 'The Rime Of The Ancient Mariner' " "Wait a minute, does he know that you hate poetry?" "No," said Emily warily. "Then he was probably just trying to impress you." Tricia never trusted the motivations of single men.

Lorraine peeked in the door to see how the preparations were coming along. "Mom, doesn't Em look hot?" provoked Tricia. "On the contrary, she looks elegant and sophisticated," assured Lorraine. Emily thought that sounded nice.

Walter was twenty minutes late picking her up. "You look hot," he said as she got into his car. At the door of the restaurant, Emily hesitated, but this subtle cue was not noticed by Walter, who opened the door and walked right in, leaving Emily to negotiate the doorway without assistance. Doors were not formidable obstacles to Emily normally, but she was not expecting to have to open this door. She stepped awkwardly in her high heels as she grabbed for the closing door and twisted her ankle.

Her throbbing ankle was a distraction as she studied her menu, but she managed to order a modestly priced option and while they were waiting for their dinner, Walter asked, "Do you know how to determine who the right man for you is?" Emily was thinking to herself, "Apparently not," but responded diplomatically, "No. How?" "You convert the letters in your name into a number, find the standard deviation and compare that to

42

the standard deviation of other names. If you find a man's name that has a standard deviation that is very close to yours, it's a match. It's simple really. Here let me show you how it works." Walter began scribbling numbers on a napkin while Emily looked on with feigned interest. You can guess what she was thinking. "Is he seriously changing my name into a bunch of numbers?" When he was finished, her eyes were two glazed donuts.

When their dinner arrived, Walter complained to the waiter, rather loudly, about his dinner being cold and made a big fuss, which totally embarrassed Emily. Then, he excused himself and went to the restroom.

Emily imagined that everyone in the restaurant was looking at her. She felt utterly alone.

Emily often spent time alone, reading, walking, thinking, or in silent meditation. She found that being alone was restorative in a sense. But being alone and feeling alone are two very different things. Feeling lonely in a crowd is a peculiar form of isolation. Her natural defense mechanism to deal with this stress was to feel sorry for herself. "No one in this whole place knows me or cares anything about me, not even Walter. I just wanted to dress nice and have a pleasant time. Is that too much to ask? Tricia said I deserved it."

By combining four letters from the alphabet, the tenth, twenty-first, nineteenth, and twentieth, you have the power to make an unreasonable request seem reasonable. This little one syllable word has towering implications. It implies that nothing has ever been asked for previously, and if this one favor is granted, nothing more will ever be required and the recipient will live happily ever after, everything they touch will turn to silver, (a better value, for the dollar, at the time of this writing, than gold) and insurmountable problems will simply evaporate like the morning dew. "I just want... " Go ahead, you fill in the blank and see just how reasonable it sounds. Emily had unconsciously wielded that power, which was uncharacteristic of her. Walter's return roused her from her self-pitying consolations. She resolved to salvage what she could from the wreckage of another disappointing date.

After dinner, Emily suggested the Brewhouse. She endured a half hour of dramatic poetry readings, but at least the coffee was good. Drinking coffee reminded her of Tim. Good old punctual Timothy who knew enough to open a door for a lady. (The Brooke girls had trained him well.) Tim thought Hamburger Helper was gourmet eating and never complained or embarrassed her. He didn't like poetry much either. He would have wanted to go dancing.

While there was a break in the reading, she struck up a conversation about favorite books. Walter scoffed at Emily's favorites, "Nothing worth reading was written before 1940," he said. "You have to read Slaughterhouse Five. Or Catch 22, that's my all time favorite." A night of built up frustration found release in her response, "Catch 22, are you serious? Its just page after page of cynical, tawdry, pilots trying to out smart-ass each other!"

That was the first time that any living being, on the face of planet earth, had ever heard Emily Brooke utter a profane word. What makes a word profane anyway? Do you, reader, ever wonder why a certain word is a swear word and another word which describes the exact same thing is perfectly acceptable? Who determined for us, which words are off limits?

Some people make use of the evasive synonym or try to play it cute by preannouncing their offensive language, as in the case of: "Pardon my French, but he's just a no good bleepity bleep." Are we, then, to blame the French for the origination of the expletive?

Perhaps profane words serve to draw a linguistic line in the sand. An opportunity, through speech, to quickly declare which side you are on. I, personally, am on Emily's side of the line, but there are many people on the other side whom I like to hang out with. It's all very confusing.

A similar tactic that I have noticed, and perhaps a derivation of the preannouncement, has application to other forms of offensive speech, and goes something like this: "Not to be rude, but he's got a face only a mother could love."

Now, of course, a savvy listener will see through the duplicity in such a statement, but the effect is subtle. I imagine a hidden meaning that goes something like this: "Look, I know that what I'm about to say is rude, after all, I'm on the same side of the line as you, but let's hold hands and step across the line just long enough to leave a couple of footprints shall we?"

Emily spent the next remorseful week remembering everything she had said to Walter and blaming her self for not exhibiting more tact. She had only read 8 chapters of Catch 22 and given up. Maybe it got better. At the end of the week, she wrote Walter a letter apologizing for her profanity. Walter found the letter odd. His recollection did not include that spicy tidbit. He simply remembered Emily having gazed dreamily at him the whole night. Where does the past exist except in our memory? Walter had his own scheme for consolation.

Tricia added some more details about Emily's date with Monte and then put Tim on the spot. "How about you. Have you had any exciting dating adventures?" she said, looking at Tim with her big sleepy eyes, a half smile, her elbows resting on the table and her chin nestled in her two folded hands. "Oh, nothing serious really," answered Tim nervously, and that was the truth.

Tim was athletic, handsome, easy going and likeable. He had been on some dates with some very attractive women, superficially appealing, that is, but with nothing solid or enduring to recommend them, like lilies and roses in a glass vase, their beauty quickly faded in his estimation. He would inevitably find that he was making comparisons. He even dreamt about that one night.

In his dream, he saw a great balance scale with Emily sitting on one end, 5 feet, 5 inches and 115 pounds, sewing and humming a little tune to a child that was playing at her feet. Three tall beauties were preening themselves and looking down at her from their haughty elevated perch on the other end of the scale, but she paid them no attention as she contentedly applied herself to her industry.

Emily's beauty, being of a form that is not completely evident at first glance, like a lush green field dotted with wild flowers growing in fertile soil, becomes apparent gradually, over time, as a diligent study reveals a lack of imperfection, combined with features expressive of a personality that was curious, impulsive, unpredictable, and always interesting, to the point of fascination.

Tim changed the subject. "Do you have any more of that stinging nettle tea?" he asked. "You sound like Benteen Willis. Did you know his wife is arriving tomorrow?" asked Jim. "He has a wife?" said Tim and Elizabeth at the same time. "She has been at a wood carving conference. They are planning to try skydiving on Thursday," continued Jim. "Skydiving?" said Harold, Tim, and Elizabeth at the same time. "Yep. That's what he told me this morning." "He's no heavier than a dried leaf. What if he blows over to Cadott?" thought Harold out loud. "Did you know that Cadott is half way between the equator and the North Pole?" he added. "That sounds familiar now that you mention it," said Elizabeth.

"That reminds me of a riddle," said Jim, who was fond of riddles, brainteasers, crossword and Sudoko puzzles; challenges of that sort. He was a very good chess player. "There were three travelers who stopped at an Inn in Cadott." (His riddle really had nothing to do with the city of Cadott. He was just itching to tell it so he adapted his story accordingly.) "They asked for three rooms and the innkeeper replied he had three rooms available and the total bill was thirty dollars." "You can get a room for ten dollars in Cadott?" questioned Lorraine with disbelief. "This happened long ago," reassured Jim. "Was Cadott halfway between the equator and the north pole back then?" teased Tricia. Undeterred by his restless audience, Jim forged ahead with his story, "They paid the thirty dollars and went up to their rooms. Now, the innkeeper offered a special on Mondays, three rooms for twenty five dollars and here it was Monday." Lorraine: "Twenty five dollars, imagine that." Jim: "Realizing his mistake,

46

the honest innkeeper sent his hired man up to the rooms of the three travelers with five dollars to make things right. The not so honest hired man realized, on the way up, that he could not split the five dollars evenly between the three so he kept two dollars for himself and returned one dollar to each traveler. Now, the three effectively paid nine dollars each, having had one dollar returned, and three times nine is twenty-seven. If you add the two dollars that the hired man kept, that equals twenty-nine, but they originally paid thirty dollars. What happened to the one dollar?"

"The government confiscated it," declared Harold. "They'll probably find it when they clean up the next morning, don't worry about it," surmised Lorraine. Tim was silently thoughtful.

"Did you know that they have calculated pi to over thirteen trillion digits?" inquired Tricia. This question drew surprised looks from the group. "Ya, the guy from Cabin 1 was telling me about it last night at The View. They're using super computers to work on it."

"They used to make the world's fastest super computers right here in Chippewa Falls at Cray Research," said Harold.

"Doesn't pi have to do with the circumference of a circle?" questioned Elizabeth. "The circumference of a circle is pi times the diameter. Pi is an irrational number. It can't be expressed exactly as a fraction," answered Jim. "Pi is also a transcendental number. A number that is not the root of any non-zero polynomial having rational coefficients," added Tricia smugly.

"What were you drinking last night?" asked Elizabeth. "Why were you talking about pi anyway," asked Jim. "I don't know. Guys tell me all kinds of weird things in bars. His wife was talking about it too. She said that you can't actually measure the circumference of a perfect circle exactly, only estimate it, because pi goes on to infinity. So the number gets continually larger but it will never exceed a larger number like 3.15, only get closer and closer to it. Then she said it modeled reality, how we strive for perfection but never reach it." Tricia paused to produce a scrap of paper from her pocket and read aloud, "Never exhaust the richness and beauty of continual discovery."

She put the scrap of paper away as she casually said, "I'm thinking of getting a pi tattoo."

Harold did not hear Tricia's threat. He was already outside stoking his fire with some crackling split pine. As the Brooke clan filtered out to join Harold, Emily suggested that they tell a flashlight story.

"Dad, will you start?" asked Emily as she handed him the flashlight. Harold fiddled briefly with the switch but to no avail. Fortunately, he had some spare batteries along, and soon a pale beam of light was at his disposal.

Harold began, "The story begins in the north woods of Wisconsin," Elizabeth and Emily shared a wink, "a group of four teenagers are sitting around a campfire, when, from somewhere in the darkness, they here a noise."

Harold aimed the flashlight at a dark brushy area nearby for dramatic effect while he was saying the last part, then he handed it to Tim who took up the narrative where Harold left off. "It's a soft melody that sounds as if someone is playing a bent carpenters saw with a cello bow. A mournful but very beautiful female voice is intermingled with the eerie sound."

Tim handed the flashlight to Tricia. "The boys want to investigate but the girls want to stay by the fire. Eventually, the boys creep into the woods to find out what is making the sound, and the girls, not wanting to be left alone, follow after them."

Elizabeth is now in possession of the light. "The elusive, ghostly euphony seems always a step ahead, now over the next hill, now through that dark thicket. The siren song leads them deeper and deeper into the woods. The boys seem hypnotically enchanted, reason and logic have deserted their minds, and they soon realize that they do not know the way back. To make matters worse, it begins to rain."

Here Elizabeth notices that Tricia is getting fidgety and briefly shines the flashlight on her, thereby granting her permission to interject something into the story. "The girls are muttering to themselves, 'We should have gone to the movies with Randy and Steve!'" This reference produces a chuckle among some of the Brookes leading Tim to understand that

48

these names have some significance that he is unaware of. Elizabeth continues, "Yes, but here they are, lost in the dark woods on a rainy night. Frustration is rapidly degrading into panic, when, in the distance, one of the girls sees a dim light. She runs toward it, thinking it to be the campfire, but upon emerging into a little clearing, she realizes that the light is coming from a rustic, old cabin with a corrugated tin roof and green, asphalt, roofing material for the siding. The others have now joined her. Chilled, soaked, and frightened, they knock on the cabin door, once, twice, three times... no answer. But the third knock has cast the door slightly ajar."

Elizabeth now passes the flashlight over to Emily. "The seductive melody is coming from inside the cabin. They creep in slowly, huddled together so closely that they move as a single entity. The wood floor creaks under their feet. Their nostrils are met with an acrid odor that coincides with the neglected appearance of the room. The walls are yellowed where the paint is not peeling. The ceiling is hanging down in places and the sawdust insulation is spilling onto the dusty floor. What catches their eye, however, is an old television, sitting, more or less, in the middle of the room. The back of the tv is facing the door, and as they walk forward slowly, a small boy comes into their view. He is sitting in an old armchair, the glow from the picture tube envelopes him in a warm embrace. His neatly groomed appearance and fair complexion are in sharp contrast to his dingy surroundings. His black hair is cut short. His button up shirt looks freshly ironed, but he seems unaware of the four uninvited guests. One of the girls steps timidly forward to get a glimpse of what has captivated the young lad. She looks at the television screen and screams!"

Emily had slowly stood up as she was talking and leaned forward, allowing her long hair to partially obscure her face. She had also partially covered the flashlight lens with her fingers and was shining the dimmed light on her face, which made it appear shadowy and mysterious.

When she finished, she quickly tossed the light to Jim. "The others come forward to see what is so disturbing. There, on the tv, they see themselves, sitting around the campfire, and a very thin woman with long black hair is playing a saw with a cello bow and serenading them with some sort of incantation. She tosses a flashlight into the fire. Instead of burning up, it sprouts arms and legs and begins dancing about like a talisman come to life." Here, Jim dances the flashlight in the air to demonstrate. "One of the boys can't take it anymore, he reaches forward and changes the channel, only to see," Jim shines the light on Harold, "Uh, a commercial, a battery commercial, a flashlight battery commercial!" Jim says, "He turns the channel again, and this time they see," he now shines the light on Lorraine, "Oh! Oh, I just like to listen. You kids are so creative." Jim moves the light to Tim. "They see the two girls, tramping through the dark woods, lamenting a lost opportunity with a couple of guys named Randy and Steve." Jim went on, "The girl that had screamed is in no mood to see that so she changes the channel again." He now aimed the light at Elizabeth. "This channel appears at first to be static noise but slowly an image comes into focus. A shrouded figure is moving through the woods, now entering the clearing, now approaching the cabin...." Jim has now handed the flashlight to Tim who subconsciously handles it delicately for fear of bruising an arm or leg. "The figure enters the cabin and the tv screen goes dark and the whole room goes dark along with it. The girls scream and the boys start to flail around...."

Suddenly Lorraine jumped up with eyes as big as saucers. Everyone turned to see what had startled her. The girls screamed and the guys knocked over chairs in their rush to clear the area. When they were all safe in the carport of Cabin 3, Tim directed the flashlight back over to where they had been sitting by the campfire.

The skunk sniffed a burnt marshmallow, nibbled a bit of hot dog, turned up his nose and ambled off. An excited commotion could be heard coming from the area of Cabin 1 a few minutes later.

Tim and Emily wandered off with the flashlight in search of other nocturnal creatures and ended up in the canoe. Floating

50

at the end of the pond, near the entrance to the resort, Tim scanned the edge of the water for any signs of life. The canoe made small ripples in the otherwise still water and the light that reflected off these, pulsed up the trunk of a large white pine like rings of electric smoke.

Emily had taken the seat in the back of the canoe, not wishing to be surprised by any scratchy little claws on her bare feet again. She paddled along slowly, admiring Tim's silhouette while he searched the water, shoreline and trees.

A bat swooped down over the pond in a helter-skelter fashion, searching for flying insects. Emily was trying to remember what Farkus had said about bats, and was about to ask Tim, when he turned back toward her and said, "I hope that bat doesn't get tangled up in your hair." "That's right," thought Emily, "Farkus said bats often get tangled up in the long hair of girls."

Elizabeth had started wearing a hat at night after hearing Farkus's warning, but Emily and Tricia would run around in the yard after dark, tossing their heads violently about and flinging their long hair into the air, attempting to capture a flying rodent on purpose. The sisters were very different in some ways.

Emily was in no mood for snaring bats on the wing this evening. She was interested in capturing a husband. "If you frighten me, I might seek shelter under an overturned canoe," she said, appealing to Tim's manly instincts to protect.

"I've never known you to be afraid of a bat," said Tim, "but what about snapping turtles?" "That's right," thought Emily, "Farkus said that snapping turtles often nip the toes off swimmers at night." Farkus's world was a treacherous one.

"You will have to scoop me up and bring me to safety, I guess," said Emily helplessly. "Hmm. I don't think I can touch bottom just right here," replied Tim thoughtfully.

"If I fall off this dock, will you scoop me up Tim? You can touch over here," yelled Tricia from dark obscurity. "Were you spying on us?" complained Emily. "Of course!" responded her sister, as if there were no other activity that she could be even remotely expected to have been engaged in. "Do you guys want to go out?"

Tricia heard whispering but could discern no distinct vowels or consonants as Tim and Emily discussed the proposal. "Just wait," said Emily, suddenly convinced that the whole neighborhood was listening in on the conversation. Possibly it was being broadcast on News 18 and three or four radio stations for all she knew.

They paddled over to where Tricia was so they could talk more quietly. "It's getting kinda late isn't it?" asked Emily in low tones. Tricia shrugged a response, "Got a couple hours yet."

A blue haze of cigarette smoke hung below the ceiling of the barroom. Small college towns have college bars and townie bars. Chippewa Falls is not like that. Still, each bar tends to attract a certain type of crowd. Tricia was on a mission that night and knew what type of establishment was most likely to harbor the answer to her question.

About a week before she joined her family on vacation, Tricia had been observing some construction near the nightclub where she worked part time. The nightclub is named the Meet Market. Did I tell you that already? I'm skipping around some as I write this, (I've already written the ending) and I can't remember if I told you the name of the nightclub or not. Anyway, that was the name. It has no consequence whatsoever to the story.

The construction workers were burying conduit in a trench in the torn up street. She had asked them how they intended to get the wire through after everything was underground. "We'll get it in there honey, don't you worry about it," was their gruff response.

This got Tricia's dander up. She felt that a trade secret was being unjustly withheld from her and there could be no real peace until the mystery was solved.

Emily didn't like bars, but she was very curious to observe her sister in action. When they had first walked in, Emily had put her arm through Tim's, whose hands were in his

52

pockets, to let anyone who might be looking, know, that she was "with" someone.

While Tim ordered some drinks, Tricia told Emily, "I'm going to use the restroom." "There's a line," observed Emily, noticing three women waiting outside the ladies powder room. "I'm not waiting in any line. Besides, the men's room has more interesting graffiti," replied Tricia as she surveyed the crowd for a suitable accomplice.

Emily looked on, horrified, as Tricia approached a tall, husky fellow, his imposing stature at odds with his boyish face. "Would you be my knight in shining armor and guard the door while I use the men's bathroom? I can't wait and there's a line for the ladies." Tricia ignored his bewildered expression and took his shoulder shrug for an affirmative response, grabbed him by the front of his overalls, and led him to the door of the men's privy, instructed him to peek in to check if the coast was clear, then guard the door. "If anyone comes up, tell them your girlfriend is in there. You won't let anyone in will you?"

The red faced sentinel stood outside with his back against the door, ready to fight to the death if need be. When finished, Tricia dismissed her sentry with a promise to let him buy her a drink later on, and returned to Emily who was scandalized beyond the ability to reproach her sister, but also very curious. All Emily could think to say was, "Well, did you discover any words of wisdom in there?"

Tricia nodded. "A classic. 'I'd rather have a bottle in front of me than a frontal lobotomy,' sort of puts it all in perspective doesn't it?" "I guess so," replied Emily faintly.

Eventually, Tim and Emily sat down at a small table and watched as Tricia began working the crowd.

"Excuse me, you don't by chance know of a good electrician do you?" asked Tricia of a man who was standing at the bar. A conversation followed and the man bought Tricia a drink and soon he was motioning someone over to join them. The new fellow was not an electrician but said he could introduce her to someone who worked at an electrical supply warehouse. That suited Tricia just fine and so she followed him to the end of the bar.

"Can you tell me how they get electrical wire through the conduit after it's already buried underground?" she asked with innocent sincerity.

The recipient of this question had dark, curly, receding hair and sideburns, thick glasses with black frames, and a nice smile. Tricia also noticed that his shirt collar was out of style, a check mark in the plus column as far as she was concerned.

His being probably ten years older than her would not have bothered Tricia if he had demonstrated more self-confidence. He looked wide eyed at Tricia, then at the man who had brought her to him, then back to her, fidgeting nervously all the while. Rather than help him through the ordeal, Tricia just kept looking at him intently, enjoying the effect she was having on him.

Finally he managed an unconvincing response, "Well, we sell these foam plugs that are vacuumed through the conduit with a string attached. When the string gets through, it is used to pull a rope back through the other way. Then the rope is attached to the electrical cable and pulled with a winch." He looked doubtfully at Tricia, then around the bar as if expecting ridicule.

As for Tricia, a peaceful calm was descending on her like an ice cold drink on a parched throat. She had imagined the process while it was being described and was completely satisfied with its feasibility.

Emily wanted desperately to sidle over and eavesdrop, but dared not leave Tim who seemed quite content sitting with her at their little table. "What do you suppose they are talking about?" she asked, glancing in the direction of her sister. "I dunno, probably physics or something," came his amiable response.

Emily's fingers worked deftly at peeling the label from her bottle and folding it into the shape of a star. "I rather think not, it appears more like an interrogation to me." Her fingers continued their origami of themselves as she looked up at Tim and asked, "He looks ill at ease. I've even noticed that Tricia has the same effect on you at times, although to a much lesser degree. What is it about her that makes you men nervous?"

Tim started peeling his label, but with no particular reason other than to obscure the fact that now he was a bit ill at ease himself. "Well, for one thing, she can be very direct, much like yourself." A warm smile from her quickly restored his confidence. "But unlike you, she has a way of looking at a guy, that makes him feel like he's taking a final exam."

This was a very revealing comment, one she would analyze at a later time when she was alone. Emily changed the subject, "What are you going to fold yours into?" "Just another star I suppose," said Tim.

"I have a little confession to make," said Emily after a brief period of people watching. April Wine: "Just Between You And Me" was reverberating from the barroom speakers. "Back when you and Beth were a thing, for a couple years, I don't think that would have happened without my encouragement. I mean, I really urged her and rallied Trish to do the same. It was selfish of me really. I knew it would never last, she's not your type, nor are you hers, but I wanted to keep you occupied until I got older. I'll have to admit, I was a little disconcerted when you skipped over me for Trish that one year."

Emily fixed a searching look on Tim, somewhat surprised at herself for revealing this inner confidence, but was rewarded with a candid response, "I have to admit a little confession of my own. I always had a romantic attraction toward *you*, but I depended so much on our friendship, especially with things not always so good at home between my mom and dad. I was afraid, I guess."

Whoever was manning the jukebox, followed up April Wine with AC/DC "74 Jailbreak" and the mood was shattered like a beer glass hitting the floor. Music seems to have a direct path to the human soul.

"74 Jailbreak" was followed by "It's A Long Way To The Top (If You Wanna Rock N Roll) and the whole bar erupted into song.

If I had a stack of gold doubloons, (and a time machine) I'd commission Heironymous Bosch to paint Bon Scott and the lavender eyed Saaski playing bagpipes while a ring of elfin creatures dance in the mists of the Scottish moor as Hizzoner the elf king looks on with approval.

After a while, the crowd settled down again and Tricia became bored with the conversation that was going on at her end of the bar. She had what she came for and there wasn't much else going on to hold her interest, and so, gave her informant a peck on the cheek and said, "See you around."

His face was as red as a Leinenkugels T-shirt as he tried to block the barrage of elbows that came along with the jeering from his buddies.

"I'm ready to go whenever you are," she announced with a hint of triumph in her voice as she approached the confessional. "The bar doesn't close for another 45 minutes," replied Tim. Tricia just shrugged away this observation and the three of them left as soon as their drinks were finished.

Tricia was quiet on the ride home, gazing out the window from the back seat while Tim and Emily chatted away in the front. She looked at the streetlights, trying to see whether they were powered with electricity from overhead wires or lines buried underground. Lines that were probably in conduit she figured, smiling. Knowledge is power.

Chapter 5   Tuesday

Tim woke up early. The sun was just coming up and the lake was a shimmering plate of glass. He fumbled around with the coffee maker until it rumbled to life with that familiar percolating, dripping sound, pulled on a sweatshirt that had his company's logo embroidered on it, Blanko Enterprises, and walked down to one of the six docks that stuck out into the lake from the resort's 600 feet of frontage.

A mist was hovering over the water that rose into the air in wisps like incense. As a boy, Farkus had told him that there were hundreds of zombies wandering around on the bottom of the lake at night and that the mist was their breath rising up from the depths.

Near the dock, floating on the surface of the water, was what looked like a bag of sunflower seeds that had been dumped out. Tim soon realized that some of the seeds were darting about by their own volition. He studied the little black water bugs for some time, trying to detect a pattern in their movements, but there seemed not to be any.

Tim lay on the dock and gazed at the insects. Soon he realized something strange. The bits of algae suspended in the very top eighth inch layer of water moved at a different speed relative to the algae below, and sometimes in the opposite direction. It was as if there was a thin layer of water floating on a clear substrate that moved independently. As he pondered the mechanics behind this phenomena, something else caught his eye. It was a dried, brown exoskeleton of an insect. It was stuck to the pipe that supported the dock. Just above that was a moist, light green dragonfly that had apparently just emerged from the shell below. Its wings were still quite small for a dragonfly.

As he watched, the opaque wings seemed to be unfolding, but upon closer inspection, he saw that the wings were literally growing. It was as if he were viewing one of those time lapse videos that is speeded up to see a flower unfold but this was happening in real time. Tim watched with amazement as the wings grew about a quarter of an inch in length.

The sun was higher now and the mist had dissipated. A light breeze had turned the plate glass into a washboard. Tim went back to his cabin where he was met with a caffeinated aroma. The only thing missing from this aroma was the smell of bacon and eggs and he intended to remedy that deficiency. He fried some bacon, then fried the eggs in the bacon grease the way his father had taught him, made toast, and poured a cup of

58

strong coffee, black as death, and microwaved it a bit until it was piping hot. Steam rose from the cup like zombie breath. (Do zombies even breath?) Thus supplied, he sat down to breakfast alone, wondering if Emily was awake yet.

Emily was awake. In fact, she was digging around in a nearby cattail swamp.

When she got back to the cabin, she got busy in the kitchen fixing breakfast for the rest of the Brooke clan. They were just rolling out after a good night's sleep and were pleased to awaken to the smell of eggs cooking on the gas stove. She served up omelets while keeping an attentive eye on her customers. When they were finished, she inquired as to how well they had enjoyed their breakfast. "Uncommon," replied Harold. "Mighty tasty, " offered Tricia. "What were those little white pieces?" asked Lorraine. "Cattail stalks," answered Emily as naturally as if she had said onion or pepper.

After breakfast, Emily went to invite Tim to join them for the day. Tim spied her through the French casement window as she walked toward his cabin. Emily was not as tall as Elizabeth or as curvaceous as Tricia, but she moved with a fluid grace and the modest curves of her petite body and average height were accentuated by correct posture to full advantage and gave her a very feminine allure. She was wearing a white, knee length skirt and light blue, cotton, short sleeve top. Tim heard a soft knock on the door.

"Good morning," was her greeting as he opened the door. "Top of the morning to you my dear," responded Tim. "Am I?" questioned Emily with a tone and expression that were mixed and difficult to comprehend. "You will always be my dear Emily," countered Tim with a degree of solemnity. Emily gazed into Tim's bright blue eyes. "I'm glad of that," she said sincerely. After a brief silence, she added, "I've come to invite you to join us for a picnic at Irvine Park. We want to take Liz Marie to see the tigers and bears." Tim thought for a moment before responding. "Thank you. It sounds delightful, but I was planning to take a walk and maybe sort some things out alone." There was another silence in which a very subtle exchange occurred between them

59

as they looked at one another. Emily touched his arm softly and said, "Enjoy your solitude. I hope we can talk later?" Tim nodded. "Good bye 'til later then," said Emily contentedly as she left. "Good bye," repeated Tim.

Irvine Park covers over 300 acres and includes an impressive little zoo for a city the size of Chippewa Falls. Liz was still too young to appreciate all that the park had to offer, but she did enjoy the zoo animals, the monkeys being her favorite.

The park is named after William Irvine, who, with a sizable donation from his company, The Chippewa Lumber and Boom Company, purchased the land and established the park with the stipulation that it would always be free and open to the public. The Chippewa Lumber and Boom Company once boasted the largest sawmill in the world under one roof.

Duncan Creek meanders through the park from north to south. From there it swings around and spills over a smaller dam near the Leinenkugel Brewery, then skirts the edge of the downtown area until it empties into the Chippewa River, which eventually empties into the Mississippi. On the north end of Irvine, there is a dam that forms a small lake named Glen Loch.

When I was young, we would jump from a sandstone cliff into the creek below the dam. Then we would swim up to where the water spilled over at the bottom of the concrete slope at the dam's base. There was a cement ledge that you could crawl on underneath the water as it spilled over the top of you. We'd crawl along the bottom of the dam, to the other side. On the other shore, across from the park, was an old concrete foundation for some type of mill. The foundation was known as "the cube" by pretty much all the teenagers that I knew back then. We would climb up metal rungs, in the side of the structure, to the top, which was about 30 feet above the water, and jump into the turbulent water below. You had to hit an area about the size of a shipping pallet in order to avoid concrete, rebar and other such hazards. All that is gone now.

After touring the zoo, the Brookes walked along Duncan Creek until they reached an old cave that was once used to store beer before there was refrigeration. Lumber and beer factored significantly in the early development of Chippewa Falls.

They spent some time at the playground, had a picnic lunch on flag hill, where there were not so many people, then took Liz to the fountain pool until she was played out. She fell asleep in the car on the way home.

After Emily had left, Tim had set out, walking at a leisurely pace. He left the resort and walked along a string of lake front houses until he reached the hydro- electric plant. From there, the road took him back out to County Highway J. A quarter mile to the right, he entered the sprawling grounds of The Northern Wisconsin Center For The Developmentally Disabled.

In the early 1970's, this center was named the Northern Wisconsin Colony and Training School. As a kid, I remember it was simply referred to as the "colony." It's history began in 1895, when the state enacted legislation to create a Wisconsin Home For The Feeble-Minded, as it was called then, and appropriated $100,000 for land and buildings. The three "objects" which prompted the foundation of the home were: To relieve families overburdened with an "idiot" child. To curtail the reproduction of the feeble minded and the epileptic by institutionalizing feeble minded women of childbearing age, and to educate the "imbecile" to the highest sphere of usefulness. Presently, the population at the center has been drastically reduced as many of the residents are housed in group homes.

Tim strolled past the buildings. Some of the older ones were empty and boarded up. He thought about some of the ideas he had heard being advanced while attending the university. Phrases like "productive member of society" and "quality of life" had a different feel as he walked around this place.

Tim eventually reached the far end of the Northern Center grounds where he saw two cars parked and people standing in the grass with binoculars pointed at the top of a stately old white pine. The object that had attracted their attention was an eagle's nest. He sat a little way off from the others and watched the massive collection of sticks for signs of an eagle, thinking about his own nest and how empty it was.

Two years ago, Tim thought his restlessness would be cured by adding Emily to his nest, as if she were a furnishing that would complete his surroundings. Two years is a long time in a young man's life and much had happened since then. Two years of working and observing the world or at least his little corner of it. Two years of reading and thinking and comparing what he observed to what he read and thought. His priorities were changing but there was still that old restless longing. As he sat thinking, there in the grass, an awareness crept into his mind. Slowly, like a sunrise, he became illuminated with a realization that he wanted what Emily had as much as he wanted her. He wanted to know the unperturbable calm, the deep inner peace that she seemed to project.

Tim sat for a long time, remembering events from his past, looking at them as if he were paging through an old photo album, hearing them as if he were playing through an old record collection. He even recalled certain smells, like the smell of food cooking on a charcoal grill, the smell of trees and wildflowers and plants, the fresh smell of the air after a sudden heavy rain fall, the smell of Elizabeth, Tricia, and Emily's perfume.

There were a few smells that were not particularly appealing, but were still remembered with some degree of fondness nevertheless, like that of a distant skunk or the smell of the lake when there was an occasional algae bloom which would seldom last more than a day.

It occurred to him, that his weeks on vacation at the Hideaway Resort occupied a disproportionate amount of space in his memory. He had spent only one out of fifty two weeks there, each year, yet, so much of what he could remember from his youth happened at the lake and involved the Brooke family.

At this point, you may be wondering why Tim is sitting in the grass, looking up into a tree when he could be with Emily. I'm wondering the same thing myself. But what voice do we have in this story? Wait, I've got an idea, I'll get Benteen Willis to ask him.

As Tim walked home on County J, an old Ford pick up truck screeched to a halt and a familiar voice called out, "Hey partner! Want a lift?" It was Benteen Willis. "Thanks," said Tim as he hopped in. Benteen reminded Tim of Father Time minus the scythe and hourglass. "Whatcha doin' walking along by yourself? I figured you'd be a courtin' that little sweetheart Emily." "Courting?" questioned Tim. "Yes sir. She seems like the type of girl that would require courtin' anyway." Benteen glanced over with a twinkle in his eye and saw a puzzled look on the face of his passenger. "Listen," Benteen continued, "this may come as a surprise to you, but... I'm old. I mean, I've been around awhile and I've learned a thing or two about women. A gal like Emily is one in a million. She's got character. I suspect a good lookin' feller like you has to beat the ladies off with a stick but they're all fluff and nonsense. I was talkin' to Lorraine, that's her mom's name, you can tell a lot from talkin' to a girl's mother, and..." Benteen had a habit of stopping in midsentence. He had noticed Tim smiling and realized his sales pitch was unnecessary. He thought for a moment, and then continued as if he had reassessed the issue. "What I was saying was, relationships are hard work, but she's worth the effort."

They were followed by two vans as they turned into the entrance of the resort. Tim noticed they were the type equipped with lifts and ramps for wheelchairs. The vans backed into the boat rental parking area. Three women emerged, and began to unload three men from a group home.

Many people from the area rent pontoons at the Hideaway. The boats are kept on lifts, which are aluminum frames with a cantilevered platform that is raised or lowered by means of steel cables and a hand operated winch. The boats are raised out of the water for safe keeping in high wind or storm conditions. The lifts are also convenient for leveling the deck of the boat with the dock surface.

Tim walked over to see if he could help. The first man he saw was older looking with an unshaven face and bright alert eyes. He wore cotton gloves even though it was 80 degrees. He apparently could not walk or talk but he had a smile plastered on his face from the time they unloaded him until they left in the boat. Tim helped the group home worker back the wheelchair through some sand and onto hard ground, then down a slight grade, onto the dock, and across a six inch gap between the dock and the boat.

As they got the first passenger settled, the second was ready to board. He was younger looking than the other two. He was able to walk from his chair to his seat on the boat. He wore big block shaped shoes. His feet stuck out at an awkward angle so that they were perpendicular to each other with the heels almost touching as he shuffled forward in one inch increments. Occasionally, he would clap his hands together with a sudden violence and groan loudly. Tim got the impression that his actions were either normal for him or that he was excited because his caretaker did not seem the least bit alarmed at his actions.

The resort owner was assisting with the third man. He was the least mobile and lowest functioning of the three. Tim helped lift his chair across the gap and gently onto the boat. This last fellow seemed agitated but the young women's soft caresses and soothing reassurances calmed him as the boat was lowered into the water. Before they were backed out and away from the dock, Tim saw the younger looking man cough up some sort of fluid which was cleaned up by his female caretaker as if it was the tenth time she had done it that morning.

Tim was rather squeamish about such things. He wasn't bothered by dirty engine oil, wheel bearing grease, or old transmission fluid, but he would have to admit with some shame that he was somewhat repulsed by the spectacle he had just witnessed.

This repulsion was mixed with a fascination, however, as he was deeply impressed with the way the three women went about their business quietly and efficiently, offering tender care and soft encouragement. He marveled at their patience. He even felt a tinge of jealousy when he thought about the care the three men received by their capable hands.

Tim felt as though he had just come face to face with humanity at its best, the glory of a human being fully alive. His conscience had been formed by the experience and he seemed to see his life, or at least the way he was living it, in a new light.

He went back to his cabin and tried to make sense of what he had just been involved in. After a while, Tim got out another letter that he had received from Emily.

January 25, 2010

Dear Timothy,

I was very pleased to receive your letter and Christmas card. Mom and Dad are recovering from influenza, but otherwise well. Tricia says hello. I'm glad to hear that your job is going well. I'll write you again soon with more details on what I've been up to, but I wanted to respond briefly to some of the comments in your letter.

You have a good heart. I too, sorrow, when I think of the suffering of an innocent child. Perhaps the reason it is so heartbreaking has to do with the interconnectedness of the human family. When one member of the human family freely chooses to break a connection, an adversarial power is unleashed. There is good in the world and there is a disordered desire for good, in other words, the desire of a lesser good over a greater good. This disorder empowers the adversarial spirit. There is an Adversary, who wills pain and isolation and whose sovereignty is increased by our free choice to damage our relationships. This I believe.

I know you have been very busy but I encourage you to take some time for yourself. Time to be still. Take some time to embrace silence and just exist. Open yourself to the possibility of an understanding that is beyond the senses and reason.

65

Temporarily rid yourself of all the distractions of this world and embrace this light.

Willing the good of another for their own sake does not always feel good or seem reasonable but it is in serving others that you will find peace. This is what my experience has been at least.

Affectionately Yours,

Emily

Tim thought about Emily working at the nursing home. He thought about his parents and Emily's parents. Eventually, his thoughts drifted back to the Northern Center. A new hierarchy was unfolding in his mind. He esteemed anyone having the courage, kindness, and patience, to care for someone with a disability, whether physical or mental, especially the severe cases still housed in the Center, as the greatest in society and he was humbled when he considered how he had been living his own life.

He saw with perfect clarity, the angelic care that had been administered to the three men from the group home, and shuddered at an image of his dead mother. "Why does one member of this human family get crushed under the weight of suffering and another find purpose in it?" Tim whispered to himself.

Suddenly, Tim realized that he was hungry so he turned the oven on and dug a frozen pizza out of the freezer. He read the cooking instructions: "Preheat oven to 450 degrees, etc." Tim put the pizza in right away, disregarding the advice offered by the pizza packaging. Tim had only read the instructions out of curiosity. He was employed as a technical writer so he was responsible for writing all those instructions that wives would dig out of the bottom of the box after their husband finished assembling a new piece of furniture, a bicycle, or whatever, only to discover that there were still several parts still on the floor that had not found their way into the assembly.

Tim also wrote manufacturing procedures, service manuals, and quality and safety documents. Veritable mountains of documentation are required to manufacture products today so Tim's services were in high demand.

While Tim ate his pizza and a can of fruit cocktail, he kept hearing a loud tapping noise coming from outside his cabin. Nourished with his over processed, mid afternoon lunch, he went out to investigate. What he discovered was this: a red-headed woodpecker was hammering away on the cabin's beveled wood siding, just above the bedroom window. It had already formed a small hole. Tim chased the bird away, thinking about the amount of effort that goes into maintaining our shelters and how things tend to disintegrate over time if left to the forces of nature, after all, things tend toward chaos, according to his understanding of the Second Law of Thermodynamics.

While he was out saving his cabin from being reduced to sawdust, he noticed the owner of the resort walking down to the dock and that the pontoon was coming back in. He went over to offer his help again. They unloaded in reverse order and Tim helped push and pull the wheelchairs back up to the vans.

Tim was misty eyed and had a lump in his throat as he walked back to his cabin again, but Emily intercepted him in transit, toting a small sewing kit. "I noticed this morning that you have a button coming loose and..." stopping in midsentence, Benteen Willis style, Emily sensed that something had upset Tim, "What's wrong?" she finished, clutching his arm and looking suddenly grave. "Oh, I'm fine," murmured Tim in a strange and unfamiliar tone.

She followed him inside and poured a glass of water while he sat down on the couch. She then sat next to him and listened as he told her about the men from the group home. "How old were the women who were helping?" asked Emily with great interest. She was studying him closely as he spoke. "Two of them looked like they were in their early twenties. One of those had her hair dyed pink and had several facial piercings and tattoos. The third was older but hard to guess how much. She had young lively eyes but I noticed a pack of heaters in her purse and she had a raspy sort of voice. The three of them combined could not have weighed more than 325 pounds," observed Tim as he gazed at nothing in particular.

Emily remained silent and after a brief pause Tim continued, "I would have guessed they were bartenders if I just saw them on the street or something, but they were like angels with those guys. I feel ashamed for judging them by their appearances." "Maybe they work as bartenders also, group homes can't pay much usually," said Emily, half serious, half teasing. Tim smiled and went on, "I never cried when my mother died. I haven't cried since I was a child. Sometimes I feel bad, like I must be a very cold person. But today I was fighting back tears and I can't explain why."

A man, talking about his feelings, is sure to get the attention of a woman, generally speaking, but as you now know as well as I, Emily's interest in Tim's experience had far reaching implications to her future happiness. She sat looking at him with soft eyes, analyzing his mood, and calculating her next move. "Take your shirt off," she said gently. This request produced a surprised look on Tim's face, which she immediately interpreted as a misunderstanding, and raised the sewing box with a shy smile as a reminder. "Oh, of course," said Tim and he retired to the bedroom, to change shirts.

As Emily sat, sewing his button and mending a torn seam, she said, "Two years ago you seemed, not 'cold,' but distant, or at least more focused on transient things, as if you were avoiding some inner confrontation." She was looking down at her work in order to relax the conversation somewhat. "Perhaps talking about your loss would help."

Tim was silent for a moment, then he asked; "Do you believe in life after death?" "I do not," was Emily's reply, still looking down at the needle pulling thread through his shirt. Then, looking up at him briefly, she added, "I believe in eternal life."

68

Tim was on the verge of asking for clarification when he remembered something else that he wanted to tell her about. "I would like to believe in that," he said with a subdued expression and a tone that suggested that he hadn't finished his thought. Emily put her sewing down and leveled her full attention on Tim. "When I was watching those fellows get ready to get back into the vans, I had a strange experience. It's hard to describe, but I had an intense dread of anything bad happening to them and then a willingness to take their place if it did. To suffer in their place if need be. It was a flash and then it was gone. It was not just some morbid feeling or romantic sentiment either. It was a peacefulness that came from the knowledge that no matter what did happen, I could always *want* good for them."

The late afternoon sun radiated a mellow glow on the wood ceiling boards. The only audible sound to be heard was the hum of the refrigerator motor. Emily was looking at Tim with a thoughtful look. Her eyes still had a softness about them but the eyes themselves had become like two dark forests illuminated in the center by a small flickering fire that cast shadows on the leafless branches and tree trunks.

This fire was a growing conviction that she was gazing on a man that she could give her life to. One who's children she would be willing to bear. A man she could love and serve, in sickness and in health, until death.

The thought of death roused Emily from her contemplation. "I can't imagine not having my mother around. I still rely on her for guidance and advice and, well, I just can't imagine."

Emily had buried Tim's last words away, somewhere in her heart, like a treasure, to be inspected at a later time, when they could be weighed and analyzed in solitude, and instead revisited the subject she had introduced earlier in the conversation. Tim responded, "You and your family were a great comfort to me when my mom died. But two years ago, I think I was just trying to keep busy to avoid thinking about things." Here Tim paused and Emily resumed her sewing. Tim continued, "I have been doing a lot of thinking since I left here two years

69

ago, and I've been thinking a lot this week about things, important things I mean."

Emily sensed that Tim was not comfortable saying more at this time and not wishing to exacerbate the situation, she suggested they catch a movie at Micon Cinemas. "There's a science fiction film playing in town. We could get something to eat first and catch the 8 o'clock showing." "Dinner and a movie. Sounds classic," said Tim agreeably.

Neither Emily nor Tim were very particular when it came to dining but Tim was in the mood for something out of the ordinary. He suggested Asian cuisine and Emily acquiesced but Tim noticed her hesitation and asked, "What did you have in mind?" "Well, I was just thinking maybe we could go to Pizza Del Re," said Emily with a nonchalant tone that indicated there was an ulterior motive behind her suggestion. "You want to return to the scene of the crime, huh?" questioned Tim, acknowledging Emily's real purpose for preferring a pizza buffet to a quiet oriental atmosphere. Her response sent an electric current arcing across his vertebrae. "You might find that the crime is no longer objectionable to the victim," she said.

It was the parking lot of Pizza Del Re where the infamous kiss of excessive passion and duration had occurred, of which I have previously made mention. Emily was in uncharted waters and was operating on the premise that desperate times call for desperate measures, her desperate measures only being so by contrast to her normally reserved character. Tim found desperate times Emily quite intriguing, like a favorite album that you just never get tired of listening to, but then one day you play the B side and discover new lyrics, beats, harmonies, and rhythms you never knew existed.

If modern décor, ambiance, an expansive wine list and sterility are what you crave when dining out, then keep driving when you see the faded Pizza Del Re sign on the old brick building, and the crown, hanging like a halo over the second "e"

The crowd inside will not miss you. They are there because Pizza Del Re is a timeless place where you can relax and be yourself. Where children's laughter seems to lift the low

70

ceiling to an ordinary height and where the food is consistently good enough to overshadow any shortcomings of the facility.

Tim and Emily sat in a booth. Emily was eating a salad with both black and green olives on it. Tim started out with cream of mushroom soup. Despite the cafeteria atmosphere, it was very intimate. The noise made it impossible for anyone to listen in on their conversation, yet it wasn't so loud that they couldn't hear each other.

During their last visit, years ago, Emily could not help but notice in Tim's distracted, restless, wandering look a thinly veiled attempt not to be noticing the waitresses as they scampered about. Tonight, there was sincerity in Tim's eyes that made Emily feel like she was the only relevant person in his world. It stirred a feeling inside her that she found alarming yet agreeable.

Tim had tuned in the Emily show and entertained himself with the seemingly infinite array of facial expression that was her most fascinating attribute.

After a nostalgic dinner, they emerged to a bustling parking lot, nothing like the moonlit solitude that had greeted them the last time, so Tim thought it best not to engage in any criminal activity until they got to the movie theatre.

They settled into their seats, armed with enough popcorn to decorate the National Christmas Tree, and just before the previews ended, an elderly couple sat right behind them. This couple was hard of hearing and thought they were whispering but were talking loud enough for half the theatre to hear.

"We should have sat back farther," said the elderly gentlemen after a couple of minutes, "my neck will be sore by the end of the show." "You'll be fine, just slide down in your chair a little bit," suggested his wife. "Shoulda sat closer to the loudspeaker anyhow." "If you would stop whispering so much, you might be able to hear better." "Whispering?" came an audible remark from somewhere behind them but the old couple did not seem to hear the comment.

Part way into the show, the loud sound of an intense action scene drowned out the discussion that was surely continuing behind them, but as the obligatory destruction subsided, Emily could hear the conversation again.

"Who's that actress? She looks familiar," asked the old feller. "That's Juliette Lewis. Now hush," replied his wife. "Can't be. Juliette Lewis was the young girl in that Christmas Vacation movie we saw last year." "That was a video tape we saw, now stop interrupting." "I know it was a video tape. What's that got to do with anything? Juliette Lewis is a young girl." "It was an old video tape you old fool. That movie was recorded in the late 80's. She's older now."

There was a brief respite from the running commentary while the old gent went to the restroom, but as soon as he returned, and was seated, the analysis resumed, "The ticket man said Juliette Lewis is not in this movie." "Well, it sure looks like her." And so it went.

Emily had a diminishingly small tolerance for comfortably ambiguous sermons or politically correct speeches, but movie theatre distractions by seasoned citizens, were not only tolerated, they added to the entertainment value of the whole experience in her estimation.

While Emily kept one ear on the conversation going on behind them, and one ear on the film, Tim was thinking mostly of Emily. "What did she mean, 'You might find that the crime is no longer objectionable to the victim,'" thought Tim. It seemed clear enough when she said it, but now he was in doubt as to what she implied by it.

Part way through the movie, Emily had placed her hand on the armrest of Tim's seat. Was she inviting Tim's hand? His dread of being involved in another embarrassing scene weighed heavily on his mind and seemed to paralyze him from taking her hand in his.

Emily was indeed making advances, but moderation and propriety were so ingrained in her nature, she had only a limited array of tactics at her disposal.

As the movie's plot unfolded, predictable as it was, a distant thunder could be heard, quiet at first, but with a gradual increasing intensity, a strange and interesting development, considering that the scene at that moment, depicted a bright sunrise, a cloudless day, and the sound of thunder was at odds with the general context of the dialogue at that point.

Emily and Tim soon realized that the source of the thunder was exactly one seat behind them. The old cussgaffer had fallen asleep, bless his dear heart.

Tim and Emily emerged from Micon with a greater appreciation for the entertainment potential of science fiction, but with some frustration at the barrier that seemed to have arisen between the two of them.

Arriving back at the Hideaway somewhat late, they said good night. "Is this good night then, Timothy Vincy? It is getting rather late," said Emily as she got out of Tim's car at Cabin 6. This seemed a verbal version of the hand on the armrest, with the same result. "I'll walk you to your cabin," responded Tim, with no discernible inflection in his voice. They walked slowly, stalling for time, hoping that something would happen, but neither one knowing what that something should be.

At her cabin, Emily hesitated, turned slightly toward Tim, but without making eye contact, said, "Thank you for a splendid evening," gave him a quick peck on the cheek and turned toward the door saying over her shoulder, "sleep well my love."

Tim watched her until she vanished into the cabin, and then turned with satisfaction toward his own door. Before he reached that door however, he was ambushed by pride and doubt such that his last thought before he fell asleep that night fell along the line, "What does she mean 'my love'?"

Chapter 6 Wednesday

Wednesday morning was chilly enough to reach the dew point and tiny droplets of water clung to the blades of grass in the yards. Dew stuck to spider webs on trees near the lake, giving testimony to both their strength and intricate beauty. Dew covered the vinyl pontoon boat seats on which families would relax later in the day. Dew beckoned children to draw smiley faces on car windows, and it gave tents and sleeping bags a wet, clammy feel.

As Emily sat in the dining room of Cabin 3, finishing her breakfast and admiring the scene outside the window, Tim knocked lightly on the screen door.

"I came to bid you adieu, I have to return to work briefly to meet a deadline," said Tim as Emily answered the knock. He was pleased to see Emily's crestfallen expression at this news, for he hoped that he would be missed. "I will return tomorrow morning, unencumbered by worldly concerns, and ready to relax for the rest of the week." "Must you really go back?" said Emily, looking down with an enticingly sad, pouting expression that caused Tim to briefly consider quitting his job. "I really need to," he replied more seriously. Emily suddenly looked up at Tim, with a faint smile forming on her lips and a dewdrop twinkle in her eye, she said, "Can Trish and I sleep in your cabin tonight?" "As long as you don't leave any unmentionables lying about to scandalize me upon my return," answered Tim.

As Tim drove back to Minneapolis, he felt empty. It was an emptiness that had been his unwelcome companion these last few years, but this companion had excused himself and parted company when Tim had arrived at the Hideaway, finding the place utterly uninhabitable for a spectral being such as him self. Now that Tim was returning, if only temporarily, to his normal routine, this phantom friend made his wraithlike presence felt more keenly than ever. Leaving Emily made him feel that way and he realized to what degree that diminutive, gentle, elusive creature had gained proprietorship over his heart.

Far away, on the very edge of his consciousness, an idea appeared, infinitesimally small at first, barely visible, a speck on the horizon, it began to slowly expand, like a singularity, as details were added, until a mushroom cloud exploded into view.

Tim gazed at the spectacle, admiring its scope and grandeur, analyzing its potential and considering its implications. All that was needed now was a will to execute the plan and bring it all to fruition.

Over the years, Emily had slept in every cabin but 5 and 6, Maple and Jack Pine. The Brooke family always reserved the White Pine in August, but in December of 2005, they had stayed in Birch. They were spending Christmas Day with Emily's Aunt and Uncle in Stillwater and decided to stay at the Hideaway, only an hour drive, instead of crowding the relatives. They stayed almost a week and enjoyed some winter activities.

Emily found the resort absolutely enchanting in the winter. After seeing the cabins and trees and lake, always from an August perspective, it seemed almost unreal to find all these familiar sights covered in snow and ice.

The three girls walked the shoreline, inspecting the ice formations that clung to rocks and hung from tree branches, and they studied the air bubbles frozen in the ice that covered the lake. Lying on the ice with their faces just inches from the surface, it was like gazing at a glass encased galaxy.

Emily forgot her skates but was able to borrow some from the resort owners who kept an assortment of sizes on hand. The Brooke girls had skated on Zamboni smoothed, man made rinks in Milwaukee, but lake skating was a different experience. The ice would sometimes crack with a thunderous groan and quake beneath their feet, leaving a small trench to catch a skate in if they weren't careful. She skated until her ankles ached and then joined Harold, who was ice fishing.

Emily and her father sat on upside down 5 gallon pails, jigging with waxies for bluegills and watching tip-ups, that Harold had set with live bait for walleyes.

Harold had also borrowed a portable Frabill ice fishing shack. It was black and absorbed the low, afternoon sun while blocking the wind. Emily sat cozily in the shack, feeling that her whole world had been pleasantly reduced to a seven-inch hole in the ice and the possibility of pulling a fish through it. As she focused her attention on the monofilament line that threaded its way through the hole, she suddenly saw it twitch slightly and felt a small tug.

Years later, Harold and Lorraine would find a picture of a rosy cheeked and beaming young Emily, standing on the ice, wearing a sky blue ski jacket and tassled knit hat, holding up her trophy, a six inch perch.

The Brookes spent one day downhill skiing, snowboarding, and snowtubing at Christie Mountain, in the Blue Hills, only an hour drive, and Emily had never slept so soundly, before or since, as she did that night, the fresh air and exercise combining to produce the sedating effect.

They slept in the following day and then the family went shopping. They finished making their purchases in time for a horse drawn wagon ride through downtown Chippewa Falls and then Irvine Park which is lit up every year with more than 100,000 lights and displays replicating the city's early history.

At 3 a.m. the next morning, Emily awoke and stumbled to the kitchen for a drink of water. She noticed that the power was out so instead of returning to bed, she slipped on a light jacket and went out to ascertain whether the other cabins had lights. A heavy wet snow had fallen. The snow muffled sound, which made the resort eerily quiet. It gave the grounds a fresh, clean look and bent white pine branches to their limit.

Emily walked about the resort, breathing in the cold air. She could see that, not only the other cabins, but also the homes along the south shore were dark and wondered if anyone had called the power company. Then she noticed a very strange light, with an accompanying sound that was stranger still, coming from the small wooded area across the pond. Her curiosity, combined with the cold, erased any residual sleepiness she felt.

She decided to investigate, so she walked around the pond, and down the road to the source of the phenomena. There was the downed power line that was responsible for her power outage. It was lying on the blacktop, sizzling and hissing.

77

Occasionally, it would arc in the woods, threateningly, and light up the snow and trees with a flash. The sound, the light, and the smell of burnt asphalt impressed a dread awe on her senses. Emily stayed a safe distance away. She had formed a profound new respect for electron flow and the electro-motive force.

Emily soon realized the potential hazard that the line posed as it rose from the road to the power pole at an angle. A car could easily run into it. She would have to wait and make sure no one did run into it.

She had already been outside for half an hour by this time, with only thin pajamas and a light jacket on. Running back to the cabin to get help or grab a phone, (and a heavier coat) would take some time and what if a car came along while she was gone? Emily saw no other solution to the problem except to maintain her icy vigil until someone came along.

Another half hour went by. Emily was hopping up and down to keep warm when a set of headlights turned from Highway J onto 167th Street.

Imagine driving home at 4 a.m., in late December, and seeing a young woman hopping around in her pajamas in the middle of the road, then waving her arms frantically for you to stop. She must have appeared to be harmless enough, because the driver of the car did stop. After an explanation and seeing the downed line for himself, he was very thankful and called the sheriff on his cell phone. The road was soon blocked off, the power company notified, and Emily was back in bed before anyone even knew she was missing.

Later that morning, she awoke to Lorraine's gentle urging to get ready to go to Stillwater. "Wake up honey. We need to get going. Portia would like us there at 10 you know, and oh, the power is out so there's no water or heat. Your father was up early and noticed we had no electricity so he called the power company and turned on the oven. There's a jug of water to wash up with in the kitchen. Trish! Where's Trish?" Lorraine's voice trailed off as Emily drug herself out of bed.

Before getting into the car, Emily paused.

In the distance, a snowmobile (snow machine for you readers from Alaska) could be heard zipping across the lake. A branch cracked, a chickadee flitted by and a heavy clump of snow fell from a branch with a muffled thump.

As she climbed into the back seat Elizabeth said, "You look tired. Didn't you sleep well?"

Harold turned left out of the driveway of the Hideaway and encountering the blocked road, exclaimed, "Well, what do you know? The power line went down right here!" "Good thing you called right away this morning dear," said Lorraine proudly. Emily smiled and closed her eyes while he turned around to go out the other way.

That was the year Emily stayed in Birch.

After Elizabeth and Jim married, they began renting Cabin 4, (Cedar). Emily would sometimes sleep in the spare bed of their cabin just for a change.

In the fall of 2009, the first week of October, the Brookes had stayed in the Spruce Cabin. It was a last minute reservation and that was the only 2 bedroom cabin available. They had a funeral to attend in Minneapolis, Clare's funeral. Harold could only get two days off work but Emily, Tricia, and Lorraine stayed a week and consoled Tim as best they could. They saw him every day that week either in Minneapolis or at the Hideaway and their support was priceless to Tim.

All of nature seemed to be in mourning that week. The lake took on a darker hue as the sun's arc was now drawing closer to the horizon. Plants were dying back and the trees were vibrant with color as they took a last gasp of breath before the long winter hibernation. The harvest moon cast an orange path across the still water, so distinct that it beckoned the observer to step out and test their faith.

Children were back in school and so the crowd at the Hideaway was an older one, and the atmosphere, a quieter one. Fishermen would come and go from the docks. Couples would lounge near their cabins before heading out to shops, wineries, or other local attractions. Emily knew that her somber mood tainted her memory of that week, and she longed to return in the fall again sometime, with a different frame of mind.

Staying in Jack Pine would be a consolation. Still, Emily was rather vexed at having to spend the next 24 hours without Tim. That left just two days and then they would be separated by 350 miles again. She needed something to take her mind off this situation so she went to *borrow* Lydia for a while.

Emily had amassed a small fortune, babysitting neighborhood children, in her teenage years, and Lydia's parents sensed almost right away that Emily was well qualified to escort their only child around the resort. Lydia had an empty nature scavenger hunt bag so the two went exploring.

As they scavenged about, Lydia pointed out a small round hole, about eye level for her, in one of the sizable maple trees. Having had this curiosity brought to her attention, Emily noticed that some of the other maples had the same type of hole, and not only that, but some trees had a small defect which had the appearance of a hole that the tree bark had grown over and filled in.

After speculating about insects, woodpeckers, and humans as potential causes, Emily espied Benteen Willis sitting at his picnic table, on which was deposited a large pile of pennies, giving Emily and Lydia a second and more intriguing reason to talk with the wise old sage.

Benteen had purchased a fifty-dollar bag of pennies from the credit union and was inspecting them, one at a time, as he was approached by the two young ladies. "Two sets of young eyes! You're just in time to join in the fun!" called Benteen. "Are you a coin collector?" questioned Emily as she eyed the intimidating mountain of Abraham Lincolns. "More of a copper collector, you might say. I'm sorting out all the old copper pennies from the newer zinc ones. Take this here penny for example, 1978, it has about one and a half to two cents worth of copper in it, depending on current copper prices. I save 'em and cash in the newer ones." "How old do they have to be for you to save them?" inquired Emily. "They changed the composition sometime in '82, so I save 1981 and older."

80

Emily and Lydia sat down and began examining the dates on the pennies. Soon, they had accumulated a small stack of copper ones, which seemed like an accomplishment, as if they were adding value to a product.

"Look at this one!" exclaimed Lydia. "Oh, that's a wheat penny. That one is really old," explained Emily to her disconcerted young friend.

Lydia's world was suddenly expanding at too fast a pace for her comfort. Having previously lived her short life, assuming pennies were just pennies and always had been forever, Lydia now had to wrestle with the concept of instability and change. Copper pennies and not copper pennies, wheat pennies and not wheat pennies. Benteen had even mentioned that steel pennies were minted during the war and Emily said that before wheat pennies there were Indianhead pennies.

The grit reality of war, Indians, and composition metals, had worn the shine off the novelty of sorting pennies for Lydia. She tugged at Emily's arm and whispered something in her ear. Thus reminded of their first reason to talk with Benteen, Emily asked, "We noticed that many of the maple trees around here have a small hole in the trunk. Do you have any idea what causes those?"

"Yes mam. I saw those myself, maple syrup taps they are. So I asked the proprietor of the resort here about it. He said he makes about five gallons of syrup every spring. He taps about two dozen trees and boils the sap on an old, wood fired stove out behind the house." (The owners lived on site in a modest ranch style home/office on the southern end of the property.)

Emily was vaguely familiar with the details of maple syrup production but wanted to confirm what she remembered. "So he drills a hole, puts in a tap and collects the sap in a bucket. Then boils the sap to remove the water and is left with syrup?" "Yep. The sap runs best in the spring when the temperature fluctuates above and below freezin'. You have to boil off about 30 to 40 gallons of water for every gallon of syrup. When the syrup gets to the right consistency, you pull your pan off the fire and pour your liquid gold through a filter, bottle it, and hide it from your in-laws." "It sounds like you have made a gallon or two yourself," observed Emily. Her observation was received by Mr. Willis as if it were asked as a question, and indeed, Emily was fishing for a good story about liquid gold stashes and pilfering relatives.

Now, the characters in this little novel possess an attribute which I admire, that is, they feel no obligation to answer a question, simply because it was asked of them. Notice, as you read on, Benteen never does tell us, whether yes or no, he ever actually made maple syrup himself. In this particular instance, he is not being intentionally evasive. He simply wanted to continue on in another train of thought.

I admire this ability, to merely give a cursory nod to any question that requires the revelation of personal information or past experience, and instead maneuver the conversation in a new direction, because, not having mastered a command of this technique, I find that I end up talking about myself, which is the least interesting subject I can think of, owing to the familiarity of it.

"Nowadays, large producers use a network of tubing to collect sap and big fancy evaporators to remove the water, but the basic process has not changed for hundreds of years," continued Benteen. Emily tried, in vain, to steer the conversation back to his personal experience with maple syrup, "Did you work for a large producer or is your knowledge based on back yard sugarin'?" Notice how masterfully Benteen negotiates the gauntlet of questions posed by Emily. "My ancestors, I'm one quarter Chippewa you know, boiled the sap down in a hollowed out log by placing hot rocks in it, and, they boiled it all the way down to sugar to use for meat preservation and such."

Having exhausted the subject of maple syrup to a satisfactory degree, and having had a new subject introduced, Emily asked, "I didn't know your ancestors were native to this area. What is your other ancestry composed of?" "French Canadian," he answered without feeling obliged, and then added, "Did you know Chippewa is derived from Ojibwe? That's the name my ancestors used anyway." Emily answered, "My father is

82

a regular history buff when it comes to this area. I do remember him telling my sisters and I that the Ojibwe originally inhabited northern Wisconsin."

Lydia was getting bored and fidgety with all the adult conversation. So they left Benteen to his pennies and wandered over to one of the pond docks. As they sat watching a little black cloud of bullhead minnows swim around, Emily asked Lydia, "What do you think of my friend Tim?" "He's cool," was her abbreviated response. "Can you elaborate?" asked Emily with a friendly tone. Lydia's furrowed brow was her only answer. "I mean, can you tell me why you think he is cool?" pursued Emily. "Because he has the ability to infer," answered Lydia matter of factly. This, from a girl wearing a Dora The Explorer T-shirt, caught Emily quite off guard and she laughed infectiously until Lydia was laughing with her, although she had no idea what was so funny.

"What's so funny?" came a familiar voice. Trisha was approaching. "I have just been apprised of the new definition of cool," answered Emily, and then, with a sudden change of expression, "Trish, guess what!" "What?" answered Tricia as if that one word represented the summation of all possible guesses. "You and I are staying in Cabin 6 tonight!" Tricia responded with a confused look so Emily clarified, "Tim is gone back to work until tomorrow." "Ok, that sounds cool." Emily and Lydia exchanged a knowing glance. "No, no, no, not cool. It's exciting. We have never stayed in that cabin before!" said Emily. "Ok, that sounds exciting," said the agreeable if not enthusiastic Tricia, then added, "Let's put our stuff in there and then get ready to go to Big Falls for the afternoon." Emily thought Big Falls was a splendid idea. The weather was accommodating and going somewhere could make the time go more quickly while Tim was gone.

Big Falls is an area about ten miles south of Lake Wissota, where large rocks have interrupted the flow of the Eau Claire River and created sandy beaches, swimming holes, and smaller various falls and rapids. There are also hiking trails up and down the river.

In Cabin 6, Emily was just saying from the living room, "Now we need to be respectful and not disturb things too much. Tim's belongings are still in here and..." when her remonstration was interrupted by Tricia, who was in the bedroom, "Hey, I found some of your old letters in the nightstand!" "Tricia Brooke!" exclaimed Emily with a special intonation that she reserved for her younger sister.

Here is the letter that she was reading:

August 30, 2010

My Dear Timothy

We have just recently returned from our week at the Hideaway. We had a great time but it's just not the same without you and guess what, the folks that stayed in Cabin 6 said they were not able to return next year. Maybe you could take some time off work and stay there for the week next summer?

In your last letter, you wondered what my hopes and dreams were. My hope is in a community of self-giving love and receptivity, free from the discord of self-interest. A city where everyone sings with one accord and all wills are aligned to one purpose.

A will to which all can aspire must be perfect and infinite. With our limited human capacity, we can only search for this perfect will, or truth, but are obliged to do so with a passion and without being predisposed to finding what we want to find.

I believe that, a man and woman bound by the marriage covenant, a gift of oneself to the other, and committed to raising children, is the essential building block of civilization. The man and woman need not agree totally on how to achieve the goal, but they should agree on what the goal is. This, I fear, is my concern; that we do

84

not share the same end goal, or at least, it's not clear to me that we do. I truly hope (and dream) that, someday we will.

Affectionately Yours,

Emily

Emily put the letters back in the nightstand, mumbling, but loud enough for Tricia to hear, how embarrassing it would be if Tim found out they were rummaging through his stuff. (She shuffled them back in just slow enough to notice which ones he had put in there.) As she put the letters away, slowly as I just mentioned, she couldn't help noticing a picture, apparently done in black crayon, of two birds in a nest, a curious thing for him to have with her letters, she thought. The nest was perched on a limb under the black clouds and with the black sun shining from the corner of the paper. Although she did not remember it, Emily had made the drawing when she was seven and had given it to Tim. Emily had no idea that Tim saved everything that she gave him and numbered certain items among his prized possessions.

About an hour later, they were on their way. "Do you remember when Tim drove us down to Big Falls in his Chevelle?" asked Tricia as they drove past the apple orchards. Emily nodded but said nothing. Tricia pursued the subject, "You're not jealous of that car are you?" Emily was about to deny that she was jealous of a car when she suddenly checked herself. "Maybe Trish is on to something," she thought to herself.

Bill Vincy had given Tim the car on his 16th birthday. They had spent many hours together working on it over the years.

Perhaps the car represented an errant path that Emily feared.

The day that Tricia has referred to may serve as an interesting case study to contrast the different temperaments found in the three Brooke sisters.

It was a hot afternoon, not unlike the current day I have been describing, and
Tim and Elizabeth, were both 19. That would make Emily 17 and Tricia 16 as they traveled to Big Falls in Tim's 1970 Chevrolet Chevelle with the 454 cubic inch motor humming along.

There is a long straight stretch of road on the way there and Tim thought he might "blow a little carbon out of the engine," as his father would say. When he hit 100 miles per hour, Elizabeth was screaming for him to, "Slow Down! You're going to get us all killed!" Emily was trying to read the tachometer, she was wondering what the engine's rpm's were at that speed, Tricia was hanging out the window. Her long blonde hair was blowing wildly about in the humid air.

If you find it strange that three such divergent personalities were derived from the same genetic pool, consider how dull the world would be if that were not the case and be thankful.

Emily served as the bridge between her two sisters' character differences and she did so with such tact that it went largely unnoticed. Their differences were really quite superficial anyway. At the core, the three girls were very much alike. All three had kind, compassionate hearts and adored children. They had all been instilled with an appreciation for hard work, a respect for the elderly, a reverence for family and a regard for chastity, for, despite Tricia's untamed and flirtatious ways, she was not promiscuous.

The arrival of Tricia and Emily at the beach did not go unnoticed by a group of college football players from the University of Eau Claire. These young bucks proceeded to toss a football around and jostle one another as if engaged in some sort of primal mating ritual.

"Em, do you suppose any of those stud muffins would be able to earn a living to support me and my children?" Tricia asked doubtfully. Emily cast a dubious glance in their direction and shrugged her shoulders.

"Why did you ask about Tim's car anyway? I mean, I don't think I've ever said anything that resembled jealousy. Especially not about his car." Tricia was accustomed to her sister's habit of sometimes responding to a question an hour after it was asked. "He spends a lot of time working on it and racing and all that. I just wondered if it bothered you." "Well, I think it does indeed bother me. But I'm not sure why. Maybe it just comes down to the idea of investing so much resource on a material object instead of a relationship."

The football now came bouncing over and landed just near Tricia's beach towel, a painfully obvious and desperate attempt to get her attention. Tricia picked it up and rifled it back with a tight spiral, which provoked a raucous response from the herd. "Hey Kenny! We might have a new quarterback to take your place." Kenny must have been a quarterback. He responded, "That's ok, I'll play center!" and so on it went as you can imagine it would.

Tricia had played on the powder puff football team in high school. In fact, she was the founder and quarterback of the team. They never actually played any games. They just practiced on a field adjacent to the boys practice field. The boy's team coach eventually asked them to stop because they were too much of a distraction, which was the whole point for the girls. Tricia had long since lost interest in athletic machismo.

"I think you expect too much. Tim works hard and earns a good living. His hot rodding seems harmless to me," said Tricia as she postured her self in a way that made it clear that she was ignoring Kenny and his sophomoric companions. "You used to like to hang around cars and I know you had fun when we went to Union Grove and watched the races a few years ago. Not everybody can be a saint like you, you know," said Tricia with a hint of tease in her otherwise rebuking tone. "I'm not a saint," said Emily defensively. Then after thinking a moment, she added, "I just think there should be a progression to life."

During this conversation, Tricia had gradually come to the realization that it was not just Tim she was defending. Her next words were uttered with uncharacteristic humility and a sadness that was more perceptible because it was in contrast with her previous tone. "Well, some of us don't make progress as quickly as you do."

The "us" was not lost on Emily, who remained quiet for some time brooding.

Meanwhile, a small group of doe had arrived and set up their beach towels enticingly close to the football herd. The initial boldness of these females was at first discomfiting to our lovable young stags. They grouped together in a sort of huddle, taking turns staring in the direction of Clarice and her friends until the news was spread that a high school girl had been recognized. This information puffed them up like steroids and they soon resumed their jostling with renewed confidence and vigor.

The whole scene, and its accompanying theatrics, was obscured by a murky cloud of hormone dust, as far as Emily was concerned. She was listening to the water spill over the rocks with a calming, steady, rushing sound. Putting her hand gently on Tricia's arm she said, "Let's go for a swim."

Emily and Tricia swam in a deep pool and then climbed around on the rocks for quite a while. Eventually, they hiked a trail up the river and back. Emily gathered plants, here and there, as if she were walking the aisle in a grocery store, nibbling on some and saving others for processing at the cabin.

On the way home, they took a different route and drove up and down the rolling hills past the apple orchards, with their windows down, so they could breath in the fresh, sweet smell. "Hey, isn't that where we got the honey that was still in the comb?" asked Tricia. Emily pulled into the parking lot and they went in search of honey. "I'm going to get this maple syrup and you get the honey and we'll make breakfast tomorrow for everyone," suggested Emily.

After making their purchases, they had not gone a mile when Emily slammed on the brakes and pulled the car over. "What?" questioned Tricia with an intonation that meant, "What the !#?!*# are you doing!?" "That's Queen Anne's Lace!" said Emily excitedly as she got out of the car. "What?" said Tricia. This second 'what' was pronounced in a more drawn out fashion and meant, "What did you just say?" "Wild carrot," yelled Emily from the ditch.

Tricia preferred her carrots tame, apparently, and stayed in the car, settling into her seat with her chin resting on the car door's window opening, peering at her sister as she rooted up plants with her bare hands. "They have carrots at Gordy's you know." "Not like these they don't," responded Emily.

When Emily had gathered wild carrots in sufficient quantity to suit her purpose, she sat down among the weeds to rest a moment. A slight breeze set a nearby quaking aspen's leaves fluttering. She brightened and an appreciative smile stole across her face, which was smudged with dirt. Tricia smiled too, at her sister's childlike wonder, at her ability to appreciate the simple pleasures life has to offer, at her innocence and purity and simplicity, and Tricia lamented that she did not possess these qualities in the same degree as Emily.

After a quick stop at Gordy's Market for some other provisions, they were back at the resort. They both took a nap in Cabin 6 (Jack Pine) and when they woke up, they wandered back to the White Pine where Harold was tending a fire and roasting cheese curds.

They were soon joined by Lorraine, Jim, Elizabeth and Liz, all of whom had been inside, preparing ingredients that would be suitable for cooking in pie irons, on the fire. That's the way it would often go, Brookes would go their separate ways during the day, but an evening campfire would bring everyone together. They ate hot ham and cheese sandwiches, pizza sandwiches, and for dessert, they made apple and cherry pies with marshmallows melted into them.

Harold was a nervous wreck the whole time these cooking irons were being opened, filled, closed, and wielded by amateurs, as he considered everyone else to be. After the bustle of dinner was over, Tricia, who had noticed her father's anxiety regarding the hot cooking utensils, asked if he had ever been burned at the foundry.

"Well, one time my shirt caught on fire," began Harold. "I had on a flannel, unbuttoned it because I was hot, and got the loose hanging part too close to a green sand mold that had the core gas still burning off." Lorraine was nodding in affirmation. Then she spoke, "That wasn't the worst burn you had. Remember when you burned your hand?" Harold's fist clenched at the mention of the incident that really made him anxious when the pie irons came out. Harold got out his pipe, filled it with tobacco and lit up. After exhaling, he gazed up into the tobacco smoke as if he were staring into a mirror that reflected an image of his younger self.

"When I was young, and foolish I guess, I used to get distracted by the enormity of what had to get done before the end of the day, and would start thinking ahead to the next task. On one such day, I had jumped into the furnace pit to grab a skimmer. The skimmer just happened to be wedged under the pipe that is used to knock the slag off the side of the furnace wall. Without thinking," At this point, everyone cringed with an anticipation of what they figured would happen next. "Without thinking, I grabbed the pipe to move it out of the way. Grabbed it hard mind you. Well the pipe had just been used. It was probably still 900 to 1000 degrees." Harold took another puff on his pipe before continuing, "It's funny how all those things that were so important before that, all the things that needed to be done, suddenly didn't matter anymore. Pain has a way of reprioritizing things I guess."

Emily shuddered, Lorraine assured Liz that Grandpa Harold had learned to be much more careful now. Tricia went and sat beside her dad and put his hand in hers. She remained there with him as everyone went to clean up and put things away. As the two sat together, Tricia could hear a commotion coming from the swimming area but her view was obscured. The earth along the lakeshore had been mounded up, just south of the campfire ring, by ice movement years ago. She got up and walked over to get a better look and saw that it was mallards that were splashing around, chasing one another.

When she sat back down, Harold continued. "That pipe I grabbed, there was only a few people in the whole plant that could handle that thing. I could move it, sure, but I couldn't use it for its intended purpose. It was about 20 feet long with a slug of steel welded to the end and a Tee handle on the other end. Old Max Richardson used to clean the furnace on our shift. He wasn't tall but he was a real bull. His nickname was 'thick' and he was. His arms were thick as tree trunks. Some thought his nickname referred to his smarts because old Max couldn't read or write, used to sign his name with an X. The company took advantage of him because of it. He was only making eight bucks an hour and he had been there over 25 years. He was smart enough though, just never learned to read." Harold smoked his pipe reflectively for a while and Tricia remained silent, sensing that he had more to say.

"That was the first place I worked, an aluminum foundry. That was a long time ago. I heard that after Max retired, they had to change the whole furnace cleaning process and make smaller tools because they couldn't find anyone else to do it the old way." Here Harold paused again to add a log to the fire and poke the coals around a little with a stick.

"I learned at a young age that physical labor has only limited value. I saw men whose bodies were broken down at the age of fifty, too young to retire but no longer able to keep up physically. I started learning everything I could. Moving around to different departments, even studying a bit at home with books. The management noticed and gave me more responsibility. I moved to a different foundry and continued learning and earning more as I made myself more valuable to the company. Now I'm considered a lead man and do the same work that a technician does although I don't have a degree. It turned out pretty well I guess. I've had an interesting career, earn a decent salary, and have good job security."

At this point, Emily joined them. She and Harold began talking about Tim, but Tricia's mind was still reeling with thoughts of foundry work. As she roasted another cheese curd on the fire, her mind wandered. What was becoming clear, in her imagination, was a vast tapestry of interwoven contingencies, all working in harmony to produce the very cheese curd that she was about to consume.

Somewhere, a farmer had gotten up at 5 in the morning to milk a cow. The cow was fed hay that was cut using a tractor. The tractor engine block was cast in a foundry. Before the foundry could cast the block however, miners had extracted iron ore from the earth.

Sand cores were made, to form the internal passages of the casting, using a binding agent provided by a chemical plant. These supplies and countless others were transported to the foundry by trucks that drove on roads. Electricity was produced and supplied through a network of long wires to power the induction furnace that melted the iron. Engineers had designed, taxpayers had purchased, and construction workers had built, the elaborate infrastructure of roads and transmission lines. All those folks had been educated to one degree or another by teachers in schools and treated at one time or another by doctors and nurses in hospitals and clinics. The farmer had probably taken out a loan, at a bank, to buy the tractor. The doctor would not dare to practice without insurance from an insurance company. As Tricia followed this labyrinth of connections up, down and side ways, she surmised that every one in America and probably half the rest of the world had been involved some way in the manufacture of her cheese curd. In the production of goods and services, relationship is everything.

They talked until the sun was down and stars began to appear. Eventually, Harold yawned, which prompted Emily to say to Tricia, "Do you want to go watch some old Twilight Zone episodes in the Jack Pine?" Emily's favorite was, "A Nice Place To Visit," from season one and Tricia's was, "Come Wander With Me," from season five. They watched them both and a few others before finally falling asleep.

Chapter 7   Thursday

Thursday morning, we find our young heroine sitting in the family car, outside a gas station, just a mile from the cabin. Harold was inside paying for gas and picking up some bait.

Emily was reading an advertisement, posted in the window of the gas station, written in black magic marker, for shotgun bowling at The Shady Glen Tavern, as a rusty old GMC pick up, (mid to late eighties model year she figured) pulled in for gas. She rolled down the window.

An old fellow got out, (mid to late forties model year she figured) and was pumping gas when another man came out from paying, and the two, recognizing each other, engaged in a conversation. "Mornin.'" "How you doin?" "Not bad. You're garden comin along?" "Not bad. Yours?" "Could use some rain." At this point, traffic on County X drowned out the conversation for a while. Emily picked up bits and pieces and heard the words rototiller and hydro-static drive. She surmised the subject matter now involved garden tractors. The traffic died down momentarily. "Keyway's all busted out." "Just bring it over, I can cut you new one." "No kiddin', you got somethin that kin do that." "Picked up an old Bridgeport at an auction last month. Sure thing, just bring it over sometime." "Whadya charge?" "Twelve pack oughta cover it." "Speakin a twelve packs, get a load of that!"

Now there is yet another man, much younger than the other two, exiting the gas station, toting a twelve pack of beer. Keep in mind it's 7am. The three men all seemed to know each other. "Startin' a little early today?" The man smiled and responded with total disregard for the question that had been posed. "What are you old timers up to today?" "Probly stop by your place for a beer later." "I'm headed north for the weekend." "Your wife let ya get away for the whole weekend?" "She's coming with." "Catching any fish up there?" "Haven't been up there in a while."

The traffic picked up again and the two men left without Emily being able to hear the conclusion of their exchange.

The old fellow finished pumping gas. Emily had heard enough from him to embolden her attempt to satisfy her curiosity. "Excuse me sir," she said, "would you be able to provide any additional information regarding that advertisement for shotgun bowling?"

Assuming she was looking for directions to the tavern, the man paused briefly thinking, then began, "Well, head out east on X..." he paused again at which Emily clarified, "No, I mean, what is it?" The man looked confused. "I just wondered what shotgun bowling is or how it is conducted?" "Oh, well, you just shoot down bowling pins with a shotgun," he said, then considering that this information must be too obvious, he added, "you keep score just like regular bowling. You use slugs and you can't use a rifled barrel or iron sights."

"Don't the pins get destroyed?" inquired Emily as the whole concept began to form into an image in her mind. "Not right away I guess. They use old ones anyway." "Do they welcome spectators?" was Emily's last question. "I reckon they welcome anyone old enough to buy a drink."

Harold had returned with his supplies and was not surprised to find his daughter chatting with a complete stranger. Emily said thank you, goodbye, and made an addition to her mental inventory of future things to see and do.

A half hour later, she is fishing with her father in a rowboat that is surrounded by lily pads. Their red and white bobbers are a splash of color in a sea of green and blue. Occasionally, the splash of color disappears under the water and a splashing fish surfaces as it is reeled in.

"When we first starting vacationing here, you were what, about 6? You got so excited about catching fish and reeled them so fast, the bluegills would literally skip across the water as you brought them in," observed Harold with a grin.

Emily still got excited about catching a fish, but she had moderated her retrieval speed to below skipping level a few years ago.

Returning a smile, she asked, "Do you remember the year there was a big bass tournament on the lake? It was televised on ESPN. All the bass boats were zipping around with two hundred horsepower motors and the contestants were complaining about the lack of fish biting. The last day of the contest, Trish and I were sitting on the dock fishing with worms and Snoopy poles and she hauled in an eighteen inch smallmouth." Harold had stuffed his pipe with tobacco as Emily was talking. He only smoked it one week out of the year, when he was at the resort on vacation. Emily liked the smell of tobacco smoke and Harold especially liked to smoke it when he was reminiscing. After lighting up, he answered, "We called in the story to the Chippewa Herald and they had a nice little write up about it in the Sunday edition."

"I remember a big catfish you caught from our dock one night. Beth, Trish, and I were all scared of it, and that northern pike that cut your finger open when you tried to remove the hook. What's your best fishing memory?" inquired Emily.

Harold puffed thoughtfully for a while. "I guess I would say it was the time we rented a pontoon and we packed up a cooler full of sandwiches and fished all afternoon, all five of us. We fished over by Pine Harbor, mostly, and you girls explored the island over there. On the way back we saw a deer swimming across the lake." "That was a nice afternoon to be sure, but I don't think we caught any fish that day and I seem to remember that you spent most of your time untangling our lines and baiting our hooks." Harold smiled at his daughter. "But we were all together."

Here the conversation stopped and father and daughter were quietly thinking the same thought. Would Emily be starting a family of her own soon?

After a period of silent reflection, Harold asked, "Do you remember the time we stayed here in December?"

You may be wondering how Harold came up with that question, having just thought about Emily starting a family. Harold was wondering himself. He followed his train of thought back, car by car, until he reached Emily in the caboose. It went something like this:

Staying at the Hideaway in December reminded Harold of the downed power line.

He was thinking of downed power lines because moving a cabin might require that power lines be temporarily taken down.

Jack Pine had been moved to the resort from a location in Chippewa Falls in the late 1950's. (He had read on a bulletin board in the game room that four cabins had been moved, but only Maple and Jack Pine remained.)

He was thinking of Jack Pine because he remembered that Emily had stayed in the cabin the night before with Tricia and he meant to ask how she liked it.

The thought of Emily and Tricia staying in Jack Pine was coupled to the thought that Tim was coming back that morning.

Harold thought about Tim because he was the only person the Brooke family thought about with regard to Emily starting a family.

There in the last train car sat Emily, wondering if Tim would ask her to marry him again.

Emily answered, "It seems strange now, as we sit in this boat, but I remember skating over there," she pointed toward the island. "There was an open area where the wind had blown all the snow clear and I was skating by myself when, looking down, I saw a huge sturgeon cruising along just below the ice. I followed it until he drifted down into the dark water and vanished like a ghost. I don't think I'll ever forget that."

Another period of silence was, eventually, interrupted by Emily's asking this; "Do you think Tim will ask me to marry him again?" Harold answered, "Well, us men, we've got our pride you know, but I suspect with proper management of the situation on your part, it could happen."

"Proper management of the situation," thought Emily to herself. "I need to determine with absolute certainty that I want to marry Tim and if so I may need to bring about the proposal before we leave."

Later that morning, Emily was lounging in Tim's hammock, trying to read, but her thoughts kept drifting back to situation management.

She worked out different ways of introducing the subject of marriage, and felt confident that with subtle urging on her part, Tim would propose again. She even practiced her response. She would leave nothing to chance.

Now, if they could just have some time alone to talk. There was still a lingering shred of doubt in her mind, a small concern that even though he had said things, things that made her believe that they could a form a lifelong bond, that they could pour themselves into a relationship that would become a new creation, she still had not seen his words translate into action.

Adding to her concern was an aversion to ill breeding that had crept, incrementally, into her subconscious so that she was not even aware of it. This subtle antipathy was the result of consuming volumes of classic literature, and classic romances in particular. Her aversion was an anomaly for a girl raised in the great American melting pot, where, "A man can stand up!" as James Otis had once said, where nurture was given precedence over nature, and bloodlines were not usually part of the discussion when match making was the subject.

Lorraine's comment that, "He'll probably turn out more like your father than his own," or something to that effect, was a great counterweight to any apprehension arising from the likes of Jane Austin. Lorraine may come across as somewhat simple, as I have presented her, but she was wise beyond telling when it came to character assessment, and Emily trusted her unflinchingly in that regard.

Emily's concerns should not be mistaken for conceit or condescension. She admired Tim to the point of being in awe of him at times. Since she was a young girl, Tim had been the standard (other than her father) by which she would judge other boys and eventually other men.

But Emily was not one to compromise her principles for anyone and she would not settle for less than what she thought a marital relationship should mean.

Please, dear reader, keep in mind, relationship is everything to Emily. A relationship formed by mutual self-donation leads to an other. In the physical sense, often a child, yes, but also, proceeding spiritually from this sort of bond an other, a deep abiding peace as real as any person.

As each car passed by on the road across the pond, Emily felt compelled to look in that direction, like anyone waiting for a loved one, who had extended their absence beyond the expected time of return would do, except Emily knew that until she heard the unmistakable throaty sound of a 454 exhausted through glass packs, she need not bother to look.

She soon tired of the hammock and the well-muffled cars that would occasionally track up or down the road past the entrance to the resort.

The assortment of people Emily found at the picnic table of Cabin 3 upon her return are inventoried here: Lydia was coloring a picture of Boots, who stared wide eyed and unblinking from the paper, while Tricia sat next to her, doodling with Lydia's colored markers. Liz was hammering out some Play Doh sandwiches. The activities of the three children were monitored by Jim, Elizabeth, and Lydia's mom.

"Hola Boots!" said Emily when she saw what Lydia was up to. Lydia beamed a smile at Emily for deeming her art, worthy of recognition as a cognitive entity.

Emily sat down and worked at smoothing out some green Play Doh into lettuce. "What are you drawing there," she said as she got a closer look at Tricia's drawing. The inflection of her voice drew the attention of Jim, whose role in the adult conversation was more or less passive anyway. He came over for a look.

"I started drawing a face," responded Tricia, "but I made the forehead too small so I turned him into a gypsy turnip." "He

99

looks more like a parsnip," observed Emily. "It's a turnip disguised as a parsnip then," continued the adaptable Tricia. "The pink wooled, rocket powered, horn swooped bungo pony is not fooled by the disguise. He is attempting to lasso the turnip." "Does the rocket have an afterburner?" asked Jim with sufficient sincerity. "Is that good?" wondered Tricia with an equal measure of sincerity. "The best," assured Jim. "Then yes," decided Tricia.

Emily smiled at this exchange and wondered out loud, "Why does the pony feel compelled to apprehend the parsnip? He seems harmless enough." "He has emerged from a defect in the time space continuum into a dimension where he doesn't belong," explained Tricia. "I mean, why doesn't he belong? Why is this dimension so exclusive?" pried Emily. "It just doesn't work that way. Look, he knows he doesn't belong there. Why else would he be disguised?" answered Tricia irritably and with a sly wink toward Jim when her sister wasn't looking. Tricia's feigned irritation caused Emily to wonder if there was some hidden meaning, in the drawing, that had escaped her. There was not. Tricia was just messing with her and now Jim was in on the ruse.

"Is that an ICBM?" asked Jim, pointing to a dark object on the right side of the paper. "What's that stand for?" asked Tricia. "Inter Continental Ballistic Missile," replied Jim. "Yes, that's right, and it's buried under a pyramid." –Tricia. "Ah... now I get it," said Jim as if suddenly awakened to a great revelation. "At least someone does," said Tricia with exaggerated exasperation. But she had overplayed her hand and Emily became suspicious that subterfuge was being conducted at her expense. "And what are those plants there in the corner?" she asked cautiously. "Cork screw trunked Catalpa palms," answered Tricia coolly.

At this point, Lorraine came over with a tray of sandwiches. She operated on the assumption that you were on the verge of starvation unless you were chewing or swallowing. "That's a cute little parsnip Trish," she said as she set the tray down. "Jim, would you help me bring out the rest?"

While the sandwich accompaniments were being fetched, Tricia espied the couple from cabin one walking by. "Hey guys! Wanna join us for a little lunch?" Seeing a hesitation on their part, she added, "We have enough sandwiches here to feed a herd of bungo ponies." The couple exchanged some words with each other and came over, he being led by the hand by her.

As Jim was returning with a tray of fresh vegetables, he had an opportunity to see the couple, making their way to the picnic table, and assumed, correctly, by what he observed, that the man was blind. As Jim returned again he carried a cooler over to the table and sat down. Tricia and the women were chatting and fixing plates up for everyone and Jim judged the couple to be in their mid forties, married, for he noted wedding rings on each of their hands, and dressed in a casual metropolitan fashion.

Tricia introduced the couple, Broglie and Clarinda, to everyone, once they were settled.

After the group had put Lorraine's mind at ease, at least for an hour or so, by consuming most of the sandwich mountain, Tricia said to Broglie, "Jim here, would be interested in that theory you were telling me about the other night at The View. I wouldn't mind hearing about it some more myself. It's a lot to consider."

At this prompting, Broglie's face brightened. "Well, I've been studying Quantum Space Theory. Have you read anything on that?" Broglie, not being able to see Jim, could only guess as to the spatial dimensions he was occupying. His guess was inaccurate, however, and the question seemed to be directed to where Lorraine was seated, a circumstance that elicited a troubled look on her face. Jim came to her rescue, "No, never even heard of it," he replied amiably. "Broglie adjusted his apparent gaze toward Jim, but, at a disadvantage for not being able to see the interested expression on Jim's face, was unsure as to whether or not he should expound on his accumulated knowledge of the theory. He knew that his tendency was to get a little carried away when he got going on the subject and was undecided about his audience's interest level. Jim, sensing his hesitation, and not wanting to miss an opportunity to hear about this intriguing information, questioned, "Where did you learn about it?" "Initially, I encountered the theory on the internet. Then I read a book that has been recently published."

Broglie, now uneasy about his credibility, having admitted that his information was initially derived from the internet, still showed some hesitancy to continue. Jim, who tended to evaluate ideas with reason and logic and not necessarily caring much about the source of the information, had no issue with discovering a theory on the internet. He reasoned that even if a known liar, cheat, and all around scoundrel said that two plus two is four, the defective source would not diminish the objective truth of the statement. Likewise, if the most trustworthy, honest, and respected citizen, accredited and peer reviewed, makes a claim that is false, (not intentionally of course) the false claim does not become true based on the merits of the claimant. A scientific theory was not a matter of trust for Jim. It was something to be objectively analyzed as true or untrue. He pressed Broglie further, "What is meant by quantum space?"

Reassured by this last inquiry, Broglie began, "The theory suggests that space, instead of being a vacuum, is quantized. In other words, there is a smallest unit of space, a unit that cannot be reduced without losing its identity. An example would be this penny," here he produced a penny from his pocket, his wife smiled and settled back for what she knew would be a lengthy explanation, Emily wondered to herself if the penny was older than 1982, "assuming the penny is pure copper, we can cut the penny in half, and continue to cut it in half, until we are left with one atom of copper, at which point, if it was further reduced in size, it would no longer be copper. QST proposes that space is an inviscid fluid, or superfluid, with no viscosity, no internal friction. The fluid is made up of individual particles of space, or space quanta, that are not evenly distributed. Mass generation is the result of relative density and spinning quanta that create vortices. The like and opposite spin direction of vortices account for charge. Basically, the physical world can be described using principles of fluid dynamics."

Harold, Lorraine, and Elizabeth slipped away. Tricia and Emily were trying to follow the conversation and visualize the new map of the universe being proposed. Jim asked, "How does this theory fit in with Einstein's idea that a mass causes a curvature of space?" "The view that objects follow a curved path through space due to the effect of gravity was changed when Einstein said that objects follow a straight path through curved space. The QST model has an object traveling straight also, but through a radial density gradient. The object travels straight when all parts of the object experience equal space as it moves. It only appears to be traveling a curved path from a Euclidean perspective."

Broglie spoke with a slight British accent that fell on Emily's ears like musical notes. His voice rose in a crescendo of excitement as Jim prompted him with questions that demonstrated his own knowledge and interest. While Broglie paused briefly to catch his breath, he unfastened the top button of his shirt, as if his vocal instrument was previously muffled and restricted. Emily imagined he was taking his Stradivarius out of its case, an instrument he reserved for discerning audiences.

Emily noticed that his belt was about six inches too long. With his slight figure, and frail constitution, it was no surprise. She had an urge to trim it with a good sharp pair of scissors. His clothes were ill fitted and hung loose on him as if he had lost weight and never bothered to replace his wardrobe. His skin was pale but color had risen in his cheeks with the excitement of sharing his passion with someone besides his wife.

After a sip of water, he continued. "You have to visualize the model in eleven dimensions to appreciate it. Imagine the quanta are tiny bubbles. Their size relative to an atom is roughly as small as an atom relative to our solar system. As an object travels through this superfluid of space quanta bubbles, it moves about in three dimensions. Inside each quanta is volume, and three more dimensions. These interspatial dimensions are not accessible to us. The quanta move about in a free space that is referred to as superspace, also inaccessible to us, but providing three more spatial dimensions and one time dimension. The time

103

that we experience is the result of a quanta's tendency to oscillate or resonate. The fundamental, smallest unit of time is the evolution, or oscillation of one space quanta."

Jim was comfortable with the mathematical equations supporting Quantum Mechanics but remembered studying a more ontologically accessible theory, "What you have described reminds me of the Pilot Wave Theory." Broglie nearly floated out of his chair in an ecstasy at the mention of the Pilot Wave Theory. He responded with unbridled enthusiasm, "Pilot Wave Theory is more or less the foundation of QST! Black holes, dark matter, dark energy, and quantum tunneling are expectations of vacuum quantization! It is a very elegant theory once you get more familiar with the basic premise."

Emily appreciated that the theory being discussed was more intuitive then the Quantum Mechanics that she had been briefly introduced to in school. She questioned, "I remember reading that Einstein famously said 'God doesn't play dice.' Is the Quantum Space Theory deterministic?" "Yes," replied Broglie, "the quantized eleven dimensional structure of the universe deterministically controls an elaborate process of bottom-up emergence. In a deterministic map, every action in the universe is intimately united through cause and effect. This includes human actions, which means we can be free from the illusion of free will and embrace a more harmonious existence with nature." "Non sequitur," Emily was thinking to herself, but she was hesitant to enter into a debate with Broglie because he seemed so passionate about his belief and she tended to get emotional when discussing metaphysical matters.

Jim, however, had no such emotional barriers. He casually asked for a clarification on the role of cause and effect and wondered about the necessity of an uncaused cause. Broglie responded that causes were determined by other causes, and these again by others, and so on ad infinitum. This appeal to infinity did not impress Jim. To him, even an infinite number of causes and effects had to be set in motion some how. But Jim had no interest in convincing Broglie, or anyone else for that matter, that they had advanced a fallacious argument. He simply had wanted to clarify exactly where Broglie stood and now he knew. He was actually interested in hearing more about the light that this new scientific theory could shed on some of the aforementioned mysteries of theoretical physics but Clarinda now joined in the conversation in an unexpected way.

"We have had some heated arguments over the years but there is no convincing him that there was an intelligent agent that orchestrated creation." Broglie smiled his assent at the sound of his wife's voice and sat back in his lawn chair to allow her the opportunity to present her evidence.

"Just the other day he was listening to a lecture about ant colonies and commenting about their collective intelligence, a complex adaptive system he called it, and that it is, but the complexity is derived from the information encoded in the DNA of each ant. He would have us believe that intelligence emerges from processes of self-organization related to the inherent structure of the universe."

Emily was now bursting with curiosity. Clarinda's relationship with Broglie violated Emily's ordinance against marrying someone with a completely divergent world-view. She wondered how they had met, how long they had been together, what their educational backgrounds were, and where they were from, but the conversation would need a little tweaking if she was going to learn any pertinent personal details about them. "Are the two of you university professors?" asked Emily. "I work for a pharmaceutical company. I have degrees in Applied Math and Microbiology, " she answered with disappointing brevity. Jim said, "I have a question for you. I work for an automotive part supplier. Our production runs are considered high volume and we rely heavily on automation. The robotics, actuators, and processes, are governed by programmable logic controllers and computers. The materials are formed, inspected and assembled without human contact. Now, I've seen computer simulations of simple bacteria cells forming proteins into complex shapes; gears and valves and so on, mechanisms and machinery that would make a manufacturing engineer blush. Can you confirm that living cells are really that sophisticated? Do they really operate like an automated factory?"

"Absolutely," affirmed Clarinda, "living cells are extremely complex and information rich. Life forms process more energy per unit mass than any star. My dear husband, you've gotta love him," turning to Emily, "isn't he adorable?" to which, Emily graciously nodded her assent, "he thinks that life emerged from amino acids bumping around in a prebiotic soup by pure chance. I've shown him a calculation involving the probabilistic resources of the universe. This is the largest number of opportunities that any material event had to occur in the observable universe since the big bang, or whatever they are calling the origin of the universe these days. This number is calculated simply by multiplying the three relevant factors together:" Emily cringed at the prospect of math being introduced into the conversation, "the number of elementary particles in the observable universe, 10 to the 80th power, times the number of seconds which have elapsed since the big bang, 10 to the 16th power, times the number of possible interactions per second, 10 to the 43rd power (which is derived from Planck time, the shortest time in which any physical effect can occur). The resulting number is 10 to the 139th power. The probability of producing a single 150 amino-acid functional protein by chance stands at about 1 in 10 to the 164th power.

This means that if every event in the universe over its entire history were devoted to producing combinations of amino acids of the correct length in a prebiotic soup, (an extravagantly generous and even absurd assumption) the number of combinations thus produced would still represent a tiny fraction- less than 1 out of a trillion trillion – of the total number of events needed to have a 50 percent chance of generating a functional protein of modest length by chance alone. The odds of producing the suite of proteins necessary to service a minimally complex cell by chance alone are conservatively calculated at 1 chance in 10 to the 41,000th power, which completely dwarfs the probabilistic resources of the universe.

I showed him the calculation and do you know what he said?" Clarinda, not waiting for an answer, continued, mimicking Broglie's voice with an amazingly accurate rendition "he said, 'I know the odds are against intelligent life but, here we are, so we apparently beat the odds!'"

Broglie chuckled at his wife's imitation of himself, a reaction that gave Emily some insight into the inner workings of their successful relationship. Clarinda and Broglie both had a great sense of humor. That was a key attribute which both possessed.

Broglie felt compelled to offer the following insight in his defense, "There is some speculation that the space quanta actually represent whole universes. One resonation or oscillation of the quanta could represent the expansion and contraction of a whole other universe and our own universe could be just one quanta of space in some other larger universe. An infinite cascade of universes opens up infinite possibility." "Actually, it does not," replied Clarinda, "life forms in this universe emerged in this universe so the limitations of the calculation still apply."

Tricia, who had been listening intently this whole time, asked, "I thought matter was actually just another form of energy, rest energy. It sounds like the space quanta bubbles you have described are thought of as particles, but aren't these particles really just a discontinuity separating the interspatial and superspatial dimensions, and could that discontinuity be the essence of what we refer to as energy? Could human consciousness just be the result of being tuned into that energy like tuning a radio to a certain frequency?"

I'm not sure if Tricia was making any sense just now. In terms of raw intellect and imaginative power, she is beyond my reach, which is not very high I'll admit. Tricia would have probably scored quite high on an IQ test, had she any interest in such matters, but she had not taken any physics and only basic math in high school so she was at a disadvantage when discussing potential grand unifying theories.

She had been an average student, only because she did not apply herself. Much of the information stored in the hayloft of her mind had been gleaned from odd characters that she would hang out with, even starting in high school. Her association with them was originally intended to create jealousy in the more popular males of her school, which were usually individuals that excelled at athletics.

Driving boys insane was an amusement that relieved her of the boredom consequent to a less than challenging class schedule, of which she was more than partly to blame of course. That amusement quickly lost its luster, but she had discovered that some of the not so popular people in her school were quite interesting.

Tricia had developed a keen eye for people whose hobbies or interests or careers were likely to lead to speculative conversations about our place in the grand scheme of things. As she grew older and began to frequent bars and nightclubs, she continued to gravitate toward those very same sort of characters.

"That's an interesting hypothesis," was Broglie's vague response. Jim said, "You're right about matter being rest energy anyway." Then he asked Broglie whether there was mathematical support for his theory to which Broglie responded, "Much. And more is being worked out."

Emily wished Tim were here. He would have been interested in the Quantum Space Theory. It wasn't long before Jim was scratching out equations on a piece of paper and asking more questions. Greek letters, ratios, numbers, and mysterious symbols buzzed around Emily's head like a swarm of bees. She excused herself and went for a walk.

The solitude and physical exercise of the walk combined to relieve Emily, at least temporarily, of the growing anxiety that Tim's absence was causing. As she walked along she thought about Broglie and Clarinda. Emily was solidly grounded and completely confident in her world-view, yet, when she encountered someone, whose ideas were as divergent as Broglie's were to hers, she usually felt uneasy, almost physically ill, but with Broglie, it was different somehow. He was passionate about his belief, but he didn't seem to have that militant conviction that would make her feel isolated or lonely. Two years ago, Tim had made her feel that isolation. Much had changed since then however. Two years of written correspondence had put her mind at ease. Still, there was a pesky lingering doubt and time seemed to be slipping away.

As Emily walked along, attempting to identify birds by their song, nibbling on various edible plants, and even startling a small deer from a thicket of brush, she wondered how she was expected to: "Embrace a more harmonious existence with nature," if she had no free will. She imagined that Broglie would respond to that question with more words that made sense to him but would only seem a contradiction to her. Contradiction. Contrary to the diction. Contrary to the meaning of the words. That was the trouble though. There is no universal understanding of what words mean. We learn the meaning of words, primarily, by reading them, or hearing them spoken, in context. Our understanding then, depends on the books we read and the people we associate with. Emily esteemed diversity for that very reason, diversity of thought that is, not the superficial form of diversity that our culture seems so enamored of.

The assumption that all people of a certain age, skin color, gender, or ethnicity think alike, always seemed to be a form of prejudice to Emily.

Of course Emily realized there are dictionaries full of word definitions, but those definitions are comprised of other words that also require defining. Emily had read a book in which the whole first chapter was devoted to the exploration of the history, evolution, and various meanings of the word 'believe'. Words have different meanings in different time periods and different cultures, which makes it somewhat confusing when reading old literature.

If there is any truth to the old saying, "A picture is worth a thousand words," then what word value can we assign to actions? Actions, resulting from choices or decisions, sometimes convey more meaning than any number of words. Actions have the capability of conveying meaning on a higher plane. It was an action of that sort that Emily was looking for from Tim.

By late afternoon, the sun, which had been so pleasant the day before, a warm glow to bask in while they were at the beach, now felt more like a searing beam that had to be escaped from. Emily was getting frustrated with Tim's absence. How could she "properly manage the situation" when there was no situation to manage?

The sun, and Emily's perceived diminishing prospects, were giving her a headache, so she took refuge in Cabin 3. An ibuprofen and a dark room where she could lie down and close her eyes for a while were her antidote for the pressure in her head.

Unknown to Emily, a trailered boat was being pulled toward the resort that would obliterate any residual doubt she had about marrying Timothy. The wood hulled beauty was a 1960 Inland Lakes runabout powered by a 1975 Mercury outboard.

Tim was hoping he could catch Emily alone to tell her about his new boat but Tricia saw him parking in front of his cabin when he arrived. "Hey it looks like Tim borrowed a boat!" was the announcement that informed Emily of Tim's return and she was part of a crowd that gathered to welcome him back and see the classic watercraft that accompanied him.

"Where'd ya get it?" asked Harold as he admired the stylish rear wings that reminded him of a '57 Chevy. "I saw it for sale on Craigslist so I called up a fellow that has been after me to buy my Chevelle and we worked out a deal. I got his truck and enough cash for the boat," answered Tim, hoping that Emily heard. She had stepped behind Jim to recover from her initial shock of hearing that Tim had sold his car.

On the surface, there is nothing remarkable about selling a car and buying a boat, but Emily understood that the car represented a lifestyle.

Eventually, the crowd dispersed and Tim addressed Emily in a friendly tone, "Now we can take little Liz to feed the seagulls."

Emily said nothing but looked intently at Tim. Tim had to turn away quickly because her soft adoring eyes were conveying more meaning than his brain could process.

"Well, I better get this baby in the water before it gets too late," he said as he turned, intending to go ask about using a boat lift for the rest of the week. He felt Emily's hand on his shoulder. "I can't believe you sold your car," she said, her tone suggesting that she viewed the transaction as a sign of change and was deeply impressed. "Oh, you'll get over it," replied Tim lightly as if Emily's tone had meant something different entirely. She knew that she had not been misunderstood and stood looking at him with her head tilted to one side and a raised eyebrow, a look that Tim knew perfectly well meant: "You know what I mean." He smiled in response and said, "I'll get over it."

Tim and Jim went to launch the boat at the Rod and Gun Club Landing. Their return was delayed by mechanical difficulties of an unnamed sort, however, and it was quite late by the time they returned. "Where's Tim?" asked Emily of Jim when he stopped into White Pine to collect his wife and child. "I think he is exhausted. He went to his cabin," replied Jim with a yawn of his own. Everyone agreed that it was getting late.

Emily could not get to sleep that night. She was now positively sure that she wanted to be Tim's bride but mixed with the excitement of that prospect was an uneasiness about her ability to coax a proposal from him. She felt that time was definitely not on her side and dreaded the thought of leaving the Hideaway unengaged. It would be so much harder after they both returned to their busy lives. Eventually though, she drifted off into a fitful, dream filled sleep.

That night, a ship sat in the tranquil waters of safe harbor, resting peacefully there, when, riding the whisper of a cold north wind, a gaunt and hollow adversary, pale, thin skin stretched over a skeleton of bone, stealing across the surface of the water, severed the anchor lines and the vessel was cast adrift.

Out on the open ocean, the blackness, the darkness, the north wind unobstructed, the waves, and the water, deep, cold, forbiddingly mysterious, filled the crew of one with a dread anxiety.

From the vantage point of her dream, Emily could see a disaster unfolding. The ship, headed toward rocks unseen by crew, is now two ships. Tricia is on one. Tim is on one. The lighthouse is dark, door locked, pounding fists to no avail, then, suddenly inside.

Stairs, feet like lead weights, muscles straining, moving in slow motion, running out of time, so many stairs. Now standing before a large knife switch. Rusted stuck. A pipe for leverage, just out of the melt furnace, burnt hands.

"Wake up Emily. Wake up." Tricia was gently shaking Emily awake. "You screamed. You must have been having a nightmare." "Sorry. Did I wake you?" whispered Emily sleepily. "No, I was watching TV. What were you dreaming about? Wait, I'll get you a glass of water." Emily sat up in the bed. "I burned my hand on a pipe, like Dad did that time at work. The worst part though, was a nondescript character in the shadows that laughed at my pain. I think he caused the pipe to be hot somehow." "Why were you trying to grab a pipe anyway?" "I don't remember that part," answered Emily thoughtfully.

Tricia went to turn off the TV and lights. "I hardly ever remember my dreams," she said as she rejoined her sister, "but when I do, they usually involve people and places from my past. One time though, as I was drifting off to sleep, I had that falling feeling. Instead of catching myself, I just let myself fall. Suddenly I was hovering around in Aunt Portia's kitchen, but it seemed like I was there in the future."

Tricia and Emily both lay in the dark, talking softly. "How do you suppose Broglie could describe his theory so vividly when he can't even see what things look like? I mean, we tend to think in images. Does he form images in his mind from sounds and touch, or does his mind comprehend objects in an entirely different way?" said Emily's voice in the darkness. "Broglie lost his sight three years ago in an accident," yawned Tricia's voice.

During the few minutes of silence that followed, Emily was wondering what sort of accident it could have been, but decided not to ask about it just now. Instead, she observed, "He's fortunate to have Clarinda. She's a hoot, as you say. It must be hard for her though." The comment elicited no response from Tricia. Emily reached over and turned on the bedside lamp to see if her sister was still awake.

Tricia had a soft, sleepy look about her even when she was awake. She was lying on her side and her green eyes, partially obscured, as her long, strawberry blonde hair fell across her face, peered at Emily, seemingly unaffected by the introduction of light into the room. "If I ever find someone I love, and if they care for me, I don't think it will matter much if he is blind. At least Broglie's mind is still sharp. Remember our old neighbors? She got dementia so bad that she didn't even recognize her husband anymore. That would be really hard for me."

Tricia knew that Emily remembered their old neighbors. Emily had helped care for her the last year that they had lived next door. It had been a very formative experience. She had declined steadily for months and eventually required more care than he was able to provide. She was moved to a nursing home and Emily sort of moved right along with her by securing a part time job at the same home. "Grieving is the tax you pay for giving your heart to someone," the priest had said at her funeral.

Death will collect its due in a sudden lump sum or gradual installments, either way, every last penny, whether copper or zinc, will be accounted for.

Realizing that she had introduced a subject that would cause her sister's mind to wander, Tricia added, "You'll have Tim, and probably children or even grandchildren to care for you someday. If I ever get like that, will you take care of me? I don't want to be alone, even if I don't seem to know what's going on." "I most certainly would, but I imagine Grandma Trish will be well cared for," answered Emily, her face like sunshine at the thought of Tricia, sitting in a rocking chair, surrounded by blonde darlings, who would hang on her every word as she read them a story about time travel to another dimension or some such science fiction. Then, as if a lone cloud of apprehension

113

cast a shadow on her own future, her face darkened into a wistful expression and she added, "As for Tim, I'm not so sure."

"Really? He sold his car and everything! What more do you want from him?" said Tricia with frustrated agitation. Emily was somewhat upset by her sister's strong reaction. "Nothing," she said with a defensive tone. "I'm just not sure that he still wants to marry me." Tricia lightened up considerably. "Oh, that's all. I'll sleep like a baby tonight, secure in the knowledge that Aunt Trish will be well cared for."

Tricia's confidence put Emily's mind at ease, for the time being, and, noticing the time, she suggested that they get some sleep. She usually slept between six and seven hours and wanted to get up early to see what Tim was up to.

Chapter 8   Friday

Friday morning, the sun rose over a glassy smooth Lake Wissota. Emily awoke early and looking out the window, saw Tim messing around with his boat motor. Half an hour later, she was gliding across the lake on a pair of water skis. By mid morning, Elizabeth, Tricia, Emily, Benteen, and his wife, had all skied.

A short break ensued in which Emily observed two things of note. She observed Tim and Jim talking together in a clandestine fashion that led her to believe some sort of chicanery was afoot. She also observed Lydia and her mom playing on the beach.

Emily invited them to ride along for the next ski run. Jim and Tim would go but Tim was uncharacteristically expressing doubts about his ability to get up on skies, saying he hadn't tried in years.

Water skiing is like riding a bike. It's a skill that, once acquired, tends to stay with you, muscle memory and all that.

Tim's dad had borrowed boats a few times over the years, and between that, and bumming rides from other guests that had boats, Tim and the Brooke girls had learned to ski pretty well.

Tim and Tricia, being both naturally athletic, had even learned to drop a ski. What Emily didn't know was, that Tim had been skiing regularly for the past two summers with a coworker that had a boat, (a Century Resorter with a 350 Chevy engine).

After Jim was done skiing it was Tim's turn. Emily noticed Tim slip something into his pocket just before he jumped in. Now she knew something was up. Wishing to engage Lydia for whatever he might have planned, she whispered, "Do you think he will get up on the first try?" Lydia just shrugged her shoulders. She had no idea.

Jim gunned the engine and Tim popped out of the water with ease but began to swerve back and forth as if out of control and flailed around comically until one ski fell off.

Lydia giggled at his antics and Emily, at first astounded that he had forgotten how to ski, began to grow suspicious. Soon, Tim had settled his back foot into the one ski but immediately began looking up at the sun and then at his bare arms, then shading his eyes, looking back at the sun and then his arms.

Now, his foot is back out and he is leaning forward with his foot in the air.

Lydia whispered to Emily, "What is he doing?" Emily just shrugged her shoulders. She had no idea.

Jim was pulling straight and steady and had backed off on the throttle slightly as planned. Tim hooked the ski rope handle on his foot, freeing up his hands to remove the sun tan lotion from his back pocket, and apply it to his arms while he glided along, looking as natural as if he were standing on the beach. Eventually, Tim reacquired the rope handle in his hands and cut back and forth with ease until he got tired.

Emily and Lydia regarded Tim with admiration as he climbed into the boat. His sense of humor had been on display and his muscle tone was defined by the recent exertion. I cannot say which attribute Emily found more attractive, but for Lydia, it was his sense of humor.

Either way, Emily was smiling in an approving, if not provocative, manner, that Tim could not help but notice. What is it about a conglomeration of cells, formed into a certain

116

configuration, that can cause so much fascination? What is it about a smile anyway?

For Tim it was an indication that another person was interested in him, was thinking about him and perhaps only him at that moment. Not just any person, but the one and only person whose attention he most ardently desired to captivate.

Next, Tim and Emily took little Liz and Lydia out to feed the seagulls, which they enjoyed ever so much. At one point, Emily counted at least fifty of them flying and circling and swooping down to avail themselves of the soggy breadcrumbs that trailed the boat. She was amazed at how, after attracting the attention of one or two, many others would seemingly appear out of nowhere.

By and by, Tim shuttled everyone out to the island for a picnic lunch that Lorraine had prepared. It was simple fare but victuals always seem to taste better when packed in a basket or cooler, taken to another location, and eaten outdoors.

As they walked around the island, they noticed a great deal of erosion. Harold was heard to say, "The old island is getting smaller every year, which, considering that nature never intended for it to be an island, erosion is to be expected, I guess. This island was once a hill on the old Lester Dodge farm before the dam was constructed." Harold knew more Chippewa County history than any ten locals combined.

Later in the day, Tim and Emily took Harold and Lorraine on a ride and Harold pointed out Mermaid Island in the Little Lake. "That little pile of rocks is Mermaid Island. In 1984, someone put a life sized, home made mermaid there and it stopped traffic on Highway X while people tried to get a gander at it." "You should move up here and be a tour guide when you retire," suggested Emily. Harold just nodded and smiled serenely as if the idea pleased him very much.

Lorraine, who tended to regard such comments as if imminent change was being proposed, said, "I'd be okay with it so long as you can talk Jim and Elizabeth into moving up here too." Lorraine was quite fond of the area and wouldn't mind being closer to her sister, who lived just over in Stillwater, but moving away from her only grandchild would not be discussed without an objection from her.

They boated back into Paint Creek, as far as the power line, and Lorraine noted how much development had taken place since the last time she had been back there. Tim and Emily lamented the loss of the sandstone cliff that they used to jump off. Harold pointed out a Great Blue Heron that stood motionless in the shallow water.

After their tour of the Little Lake area, they sped north, took a swing through Pine Harbor, motored gently across the sand bar, and into the Yellow River. They went past Lake Wissota State Park and Half Moon Bay and as far as the Highway K Bridge.

After reentering the Big Lake, Tim cut across to the west shore and turned south at the Rod and Gun Club. They proceeded slowly past the dam and hydroelectric plant, which afforded Harold the opportunity to regale them with a few more anecdotes and statistics, before returning to the Hideaway.

While Tim replenished his supply of petrol, Emily joined her sisters who were already engaged in dinner preparations.

It was customary for Elizabeth, Emily, and Tricia to prepare a big dinner on Friday night, the final night of their vacation, to show their gratitude for another fun filled week at the lake. They would fry up any accumulation of fish fillets that had been caught that week, and add side dishes of home made macaroni and cheese, or another pasta, some form of potato, and fresh baked bread.

Tricia was in charge of the fish. First, she rolled the fillets in flour. Then dipped them in a batter of milk, eggs and beer. Next, she shook them in a bag filled with seasoned breadcrumbs or crushed Saltine crackers before frying them in peanut oil.

While Elizabeth was setting the table, she noticed Harold sitting on a bench near the lake with his arm around Lorraine. "Look at those two. I hope Jim is as affectionate as Dad when we get that old." "He's probably just holding her down. You know she can't relax when someone is working in the kitchen and she is not helping," observed Tricia, and then, to Emily, she added,

118

"You're awfully quiet." "I noticed that you seem distracted. Are you settled on your response if Tim asks you again?" questioned Elizabeth. After a brief pause Emily responded, "I intend to accept a proposal if I have the opportunity," and then after another brief pause, "We haven't really had any time alone since he returned."

Elizabeth and Tricia exchanged a sisterly glance and then Elizabeth said, "We'll try to manage that after dinner." Emily just smiled in response to the offer, which she appreciated. Her confidence in her ability to coax a proposal out of Tim was waning however, as she couldn't imagine precisely what she would say. Tim had given every indication that he wanted to pursue a relationship, but had she adequately encouraged him? She was surprised at herself, to find it so difficult to express her willingness.

Everyone enjoyed dinner, and a casual conversation, which centered on reflections from the past week, a week that had passed too quickly, as it always did. Permeating the conversation, however, like a thick fog that no one wished to acknowledge, that was felt more than it was seen, moistening the lungs more than the eyes, was an underlying sentiment that there was still unfinished business. It was as if there was a ship still out to sea and what right had they to leave off watching for it until it returned safely? This fog settled and weighed heavily on Emily as she cleaned up after dinner.

After finishing up the dishes, Emily spied Tim out on the dock. As she approached him, not knowing what she would say or do when she got there, but seemingly propelled along by some unseen current, Tim turned to her and suggested that they have a drink at the Mallard.

"That sounds lovely. Can I just freshen up a bit first?" "Ok, then I'll do the same. See you in half an hour." "Let's make it 45 minutes," said Emily as she hustled off to gather her support team.

"Tim and I are going to take a little cruise up to the Mallard," was all she needed to say to Elizabeth and Tricia to ignite a flurry of activity.

The Mallard Resort is 5 miles north of Chippewa Falls on the Chippewa River. By boat, it's about ten miles from the only other resort on Wissota, the Hideaway. (The upper Chippewa, part of the Yellow River, Little Lake Wissota, and even the last stretches of Paint and Stillson creeks are all referred to as Lake Wissota in a general way.)

The Mallard was purchased in 1946 by Ralph and Marion Bergholtz, who established the resort as it is today, with over two dozen campsites, four cottages and the bar. Ralph died in 1961 and Marion ran the operation until the mid seventies when her daughter, Bev Chartier, took over. Most of the campsites are permanent ones that have been occupied by the same families, every summer, for a long time. Getting a permanent site at the Mallard is roughly akin to securing season tickets at Lambeau Field. Bev had died in May and, not having any children, she left the resort to those families, who have kept the business going nicely.

"What are you going to wear?" asked Elizabeth. "I was thinking one or the other of these two," replied Emily, holding up her two options, one at a time. The first was a casual, lace, sleeveless, mini dress. It was peach in color and the shortest dress she owned. The second was a more modest ensemble consisting of roll-cuff denim cropped jeans and a cotton button up short sleeve top.

"Wear the peach and bring your light black sweater. It will be cool on the way home so it will be perfectly natural to have it along and if there are any brutish men at the bar you can cover up with it," said Elizabeth. "Whoa, this is serious," said Tricia, impressed by her conservative sister's choice.

Emily was flushed with an excited anticipation. Her two sisters fussed over her make up but found it difficult to improve on her natural radiant glow. Here, Elizabeth deferred to her younger sister and was equally impressed with her suggestions. A light, subtle, and tasteful application of fuchsia rouge to her lips and a hint of eyeliner was finally decided to be sufficient.

Emily's hair was the subject of some debate. "You should wear it up. Otherwise, you will look disheveled by the time you

120

get there. You know how it is riding in a boat," suggested Elizabeth. "Guys like disheveled," replied Tricia bluntly. Emily decided to wear it down but promised to put it up when she got there if it was looking too wild from the boat ride.

If there was one thing in which Emily indulged her self, it was jewelry. Emily liked to wear jewelry. It was not unusual for her to be sporting as many as three rings, on each hand, plus bracelets and earrings. Tricia and Elizabeth both agreed that bracelets and earrings were desirable but that she should definitely not wear any rings. I don't know if they thought that the absence of rings on her fingers would create a vacuum effect or if they figured Tim would notice and attempt to correct the deficiency, but they were both adamant on the point, so Emily relented.

Meanwhile, back at Cabin 6, Tim had splashed some water on his face and changed his shirt. He now had 40 minutes to wait while Emily's pit crew administered their preparations on her. His mind had opportunity to wander.

He was thankful to be wearing short sleeve shirts because his arms were long and he found it difficult to find long sleeve shirts that fit properly. He had watched a live exhibit, at a history museum earlier in the summer, demonstrating how the fibers of the flax plant were spun into yarn and then woven into fabric.

Tim remembered that his grandfather, who started out as a common laborer, then learned a skilled trade as an apprentice bricklayer, had told him once that he had owned only one suit of clothing until he was in his late thirties, but it was custom tailored and made from linen and wool. Tim lamented that, despite our modern technology and high standard of living, his closet was filled with ill fitted clothing made from inferior materials.

As a young boy, he used to walk around his grandfather's neighborhood and his grandfather would point out houses that he had helped build or repair. These were modest homes, owned by middle class families, but every one was unique. He saw ornate lintels and arched windows, dormers and gables and columns and other architectural features deemed too costly to incorporate into today's designs. He saw brickwork that had aesthetic appeal, function and form combined.

Tim was not thinking in terms of right or wrong; good or bad, he was just thinking about change. Work used to have a spiritual dimension. It used to involve craftsmanship, and the satisfaction of seeing a project to its completion. It used to be a platform for self-expression. The advent of the assembly line and the industrial revolution had brought about much lamentable change. The human connection between the labor and the recipient of the product has been diminished.

His conjecture was this; the "git 'er done" attitude that prevails now, does not allow for a turret to be designed into a home destined to be owned by a pipe fitter or a butcher. Don't misunderstand, Tim had great respect for Git 'er done when what needed to be done was grading a road, splitting wood, plowing a field and a thousand other necessary activities that are the engine of society, but gone are the days when a piece of furniture was a work of art and every home a castle.

Of course Tim understood that the change he was ruminating on was a generalization and there are always exceptions. He was also aware of the consumer side to the equation. The cost imposed by our quest for comfort is often exacted from beauty.

After an hour of primping, Emily was ready to go. Tim was waiting patiently on the dock. "The oars were in the boat," he said smiling, as the vision of loveliness approached him. Emily returned his smile with a fuchsia rouge smile of her own and Timothy helped his lifelong friend into his Inland Lakes boat.

The ride up the river was uneventful. Both were a little nervous and it was difficult to talk over the sound of the motor so they mostly enjoyed the scenery.

Emily's hair arrived at the Mallard with just the right amount of dishevelment. She made only minor adjustments as Tim secured the boat to one of many docks available to the public, and then they walked up to the bar.

It was a mixed crowd, and a friendly atmosphere, so Tim and Emily aroused no special attention and Emily's sweater was not called into service.

Emily had been to the Mallard a few times over the years and she always felt that she was stepping back in time when she walked in. That's not to suggest it was run down, rather, she sensed it was a place where decades of concentrated human interaction had taken place. Emily sat with a glass of wine, pondering how many sorrows had been drowned there, how many promises made, and broken, how many relationships started, and ended, how many hand shakes, hugs, and kisses had been exchanged, how many plans had been scratched out on napkins, how many embellished fish catches had been reported, how much speculation on upcoming Packer seasons, and she wondered if anyone had ever been proposed to in that little watering hole where time seemed to have no authority.

When Tim joined her with a glass of Leinenkugels, Emily asked, "Do you suppose anyone here is cheating?" Tim knew this question was an invitation. He studied the crowd, looking for two animated and interesting people, which he soon found. "I believe that fellow over there just might be."

He had selected two people who were talking politics at the bar. The man was a local mechanic wearing his blue work uniform. The woman was a tourist from Chicago who was dressed to the nines.

Tim and Emily had devised an amusement. When mixed in with a crowd of people, they would pick two from the crowd and watch their gestures, then, make up a conversation that they imagined them to be having. Tim and Emily did not know anything about the other two, nor could they hear what they were saying.

The man had been talking and tugging occasionally at his beard. A clue to his occupation was visible under his fingernails where the GoJo couldn't reach. From her vantage point, Emily did not see that detail.

"Isn't that a wedding ring?" began Emily. "What, this little thing? Naw, my buddy found this. I just wear it to remind me to

123

ask around if anybody has lost their ring. No, I'm as single as Velveeta cheese," countered Tim. "Did you mean American cheese? I hate peeling off those cellophane wrappers," corrected Emily.

Now, the woman was talking to the man in a patronizing tone, which Emily could not hear. "Oh? If your 'buddy' found the ring, than how is it, that *you* have possession of it? I suppose your buddy's wife is insanely jealous and so he dared not retain it for fear of his life?" said Emily as she saw the woman finish talking with a demonstrative flourish that seemed to put the man back on his heels a bit.

"Say, you're pretty sharp. You got that just right," said Tim. The man was now looking at his cell phone so Tim continued, "Hey. Let me show you a picture of the Musky I caught the other day. Caught it just up the river from here in the fast current below the Jim Falls dam I did."

The woman took a glance at the phone that he held toward her and made some brief comment. "That's nothing. I landed a fifty inch just this morning near Chippewa City on a Mouldy's Topper Stopper," said Emily. The image of the petite Emily holding up a trophy Musky with the many trebled lure still dangling from its mouth produced a little chuckle in Tim as he watched the man talking now and gesturing toward the window.

It was Tim's turn now, "So you like to fish? I've got a boat docked out there right now. How's about you and me try a little night fishing?" Now it was the woman's and Emily's turn, "You're not a Packer fan are you? I'm not going fishing with any Packer fan."

The man had been at the bar long enough to have put a few away and was beginning to tire of politics. He began to serenade the woman, singing along with the jukebox. Tim said quickly, "Packers? Are you kidding? I'm Chicago all the way. I even know the Bears fight song," then he sang it.
Bear down, Chicago Bears,
Every play leads the way to victory.
Bear down, Chicago Bears
As you go meet the foe so fearlessly.
124

We'll never forget the way you thrilled the nation
With your T formation.
Bear Down, Chicago Bears,
Every game paves the way to the top.
You're the pride and joy of Illinois,
Bear down, Chicago Bears.

He had not sung that song since grade school and didn't have many of the lines remembered correctly but Emily was none the wiser and found it endearing.

Tim sang with such a passion, such a serious expression, and so off key that Emily started giggling and she could barely compose herself in time to offer this as the women finished her drink and picked up her purse. "I'll go and freshen up a bit at my cabin."

The man made an unsuccessful attempt to retain her and she turned and said something as she was leaving. And so Tim; "I'll meet you at the boat in half an hour?" And Emily, "Make it 45 minutes." And Tim, "I'll see you in an hour then."

Resuming a more traditional conversation, Emily said with a smile, "I never heard you sing the Chicago Bears fight song before. In fact, I don't think I've ever heard you sing before. You have a cute little singing voice." "They teach every Belvidere grade schooler that, right along with the National Anthem," said Tim proudly.

Tim strolled over to the window and back. Emily was eager to get back in the boat, to be alone with Tim. He was keeping an eye on the skyline, gaging the sun's position. He insisted on one more drink.

Emily was wearing her curious smile and arched eyebrows when Tim returned from the bar with two glasses of beer and two shots of root beer schnapps. "Another one of your father's inventions?" Nodding, Tim replied, "When we finish the beers to about here," pointing to just over half a glass, "stop, and I'll show you how to drink a root beer barrel."

125

As they motored slowly back from the Mallard Resort, the setting sun illuminated the low, stratocumulus clouds with red, orange and pink color. The sandstone cliffs, on the west shore, towered over the dark water that was tinged with a pink reflection of the radiant atmosphere above.

"Should we stop here and watch the sun set?" asked Tim. Emily nodded. She could not have dreamt of a more perfect spot to become engaged. She was thinking smugly that she had managed things pretty well after all. Then she realized that it was Tim who had brought this situation about.

They sat silently for a while, at this secluded bend in the river, gazing at the raw beauty of the scene. Emily fancied that the sun must have been practicing for thousands of years to achieve this level of perfection. Surely, the ancient Sumerians were never privileged to such a display. Every day in the past was a mere crumpled piece of paper, a torn up canvas, lying on the floor near the sun's easel, a rejected rough draft that was declared; "Not good enough!" by the moon.

Emily cast a shy glance at Tim. He appeared to be contentedly absorbed by the surroundings and showed no inclination to speak, much less propose.

She reflected that it was Tim, after all, who had proposed two years ago and been rejected by her. It was Tim who sold his car and acquired the boat. Tim had dispensed with the obligatory rides early enough in the day so they could be alone now. He had timed the return trip to catch the sunset at this particular spot, and she realized that it was unfair to expect more of him. She would have to make the next move.

The peaceful silence became dreadfully wretched as Emily searched, in vain, for the right words and noticed Tim's contented expression slowly degrade into a solemn despondence. Her urgency was quickly escalated to desperation as Tim reached to start the boat but she was, strangely, unable to speak. Her mind felt numbly useless, unable to coax her mouth to form words. Humbly exasperated at her futile efforts, she prayed for some sort of intervention.

By some twist of fate or the workings of her guardian angel, you decide, the engine turned over and over but would not fire. (If you are familiar with 1970's era outboards, you know that little intervention would be needed for this to occur.)

This development was a mixed blessing for Emily. It gave her more time to regain the faculty of speech, but Tim, like all the men in her life, would become hopelessly distracted by the prospect of a stalled internal combustion engine. In fact, his problem-solver instinct had already manifested itself, and the romantic moment was lost forever, as Tim went for tools from a small onboard storage cabinet.

He soon realized that he had put a lock on it in case he wanted to store his wallet or other valuables there some day. As he fumbled around in search of the key, he absent-mindedly checked his pocket and a silver ring fell to the floor of the boat as he removed his hand.

The sight of this, object of her desire, sent a small convulsion coursing through Emily's body. She stared, wide eyed, as Tim reached down to pick it up. Emily, apparently still unable to talk, but able to move, intercepted his retrieval by grabbing his arm after he had the ring in his hand. She was not about to let that ring out of her sight again.

Tim looked at her with surprise. Emily still said nothing but simply held out her other hand with an imploring look. Tim met her silent appeal by placing the ring on her finger, and the sun and the moon rejoiced that all was right with the world.

Chapter 9   About Two Years Later

Emily Vincy was bustling about the house making last minute preparations for a candle light dinner. She wanted everything to be perfect and Tim was expected home from work any time. There was a roast in the oven to which would be added mashed potatoes and gravy. Emily had dug up the potatoes, (Yukon Gold and Kennebec) that morning from their garden.

After finishing school, she had worked full time proofreading books for a large publisher. She also did some editing. There didn't seem to be many career opportunities available for her and she felt obligated to do something related to her degree. After she and Tim were married however, Tim encouraged her to quit and work at a nursing home part time instead and so she did, because she enjoyed the people and found it rewarding.

Their home was an old farmhouse, just down the road from Emily's Aunt and Uncle outside Stillwater, MN. Tim commuted to work in Minneapolis but was able to work from home a couple days a week and Emily would often help him.

A few months ago, when Tim was sick with influenza, Emily had written almost a complete manual for a lawn mower. Of course, she felt obliged to put her own spin on it. If you happen to purchase a lawn mower that was manufactured by Tim's company around that time, and bother to read the manual, you will be instructed as follows:

The Blanko Mower

INSTRUCTIONS FOR WORKING
AND MAINTEANCE.

Simplicity of control and maintenance have been reduced to a fine art, and if it is used and looked after in the manner described here, the Blanko will give you yeoman service.

Please keep this "manual" handy. Read it before you use the machine the first time, and refer to it as occasion demands. It gives you in concentrated form, the vast store of knowledge which we have accumulated of how best to mow with the Blanko and how to look after it.

And so it went in like fashion, presenting all the necessary technical information and concluding with a conclusion, 8 pages later.

CONCLUSION

A minimum of service will be required with your Blanko. In the unlikely event of difficulties arising which are not capable of simple remedy by referring to this manual, get in touch with your dealer, or in case of difficulty, with the Blanko Service Department, of which addresses are given opposite.
By following this course, you will find prompt, courteous and efficient service available always at reasonable charges.

Finally, we wish to assure you that your satisfaction with your Blanko is our permanent interest, forming part, as it does, of a world-wide Blanko goodwill.

Emily, by some irrevocable misfortune, had been conceived and born in the wrong time and place. Her habits, manners, dress, speech, and tastes were better suited to late nineteenth century England.

Of this anomaly, I admit some sympathy of understanding and commiseration. I sometimes think that I should have been a teenager in the late 1950's, although I was conceived and born in precisely the correct geographic location.

I wonder though, had I been a teenager in the 1950's, and as I torqued some bolts on my flat head Ford powered rail job, would I have looked back longingly at the steam engine era?

Emily was particularly eager for Tim to try the side dish, Chicken Of The Woods mushroom, fried in olive oil and lightly salted, which she had found growing on the base of an oak tree near the back of their property which covered forty acres. Thirty

130

acres were tillable farmland and they rented that to a nearby farmer.

She had also attempted to bake a loaf of bread. Emily's baking skills could best be described as improving. With perfection her goal for this particular meal, and her experiment falling short of the mark, she had borrowed a loaf from her Aunt, Portia March.

Portia was Lorraine's older sister by three years, that is, she had ridden planet earth around the sun three times already before Lorraine came along. She was married to Henry March and the two of them had four children, the youngest being a year older than Emily. The March family lived on a small hobby farm and Henry was employed as a machinist.

Portia not only baked her own bread, but she ground the flour in a hand cranked grain mill. "I buy the wheat, which is sometimes called wheat berries, but they aren't berries at all they are the seed, a living entity," explained Portia to Emily, "and when you grind it dead, it begins to decompose. The flavor and nutrition diminish over time so I grind it and use it the same day. The stuff you buy in the store has been sitting around a while so they have to enrich it to put the nutrition back into it and sometimes bleach it to keep it from getting rancid." Emily took this as a positively frightening revelation. Portia, noticing the startled look on her apprentice's face, said reassuringly, "Don't worry dearie, our bodies seem to have adjusted to store flour and preservative filled bread. People are living longer than ever after all. But if you want the good stuff, you grind your own."

You may think that Aunt March's hand ground flour was the secret to her manna from heavenly bread but that was not it. She also used yeast that had been cultivated and handed down, from generation to generation, like a family heirloom.

Tim and Emily got their supply of fresh milk from Henry and Portia, or rather from Deidra, their Dexter cow. Deidra was a good homesteading cow. She was smaller than other breeds and a good forager and so less costly to keep, but still capable of supplying even a large household with enough milk.

Emily had learned all about keeping laying hens from visits to the March farm as she was growing up. A chicken coop was one of the first projects Tim completed after they settled on the property.

Emily was at odds with most the rest of American society with regard to keeping pets. While she enjoyed animals, she much preferred them outdoors, "Where they belong," as she would say. She thought it ironic that so much effort and expense, was directed toward a family's dwelling, to shelter them from the cold and heat; the sun and rain; insects and animals, but then an animal was intentionally brought inside to live there. Chickens suited her nicely because they were amusing, stayed outside, easy to care for, and the investment of resources directed toward their maintenance yielded a tasty return in eggs, or as Tim's father called them, cackle berries.

They had a mix of Buff Orpingtons, Plymouth Barred Rocks, and Ameraucana, breeds that laid colorful eggs and had a good temperament.

Emily's solitary pet venture occurred when she was 5 years old. Harold had won her a goldfish at the state fair and she named it Whackadoo. Whackadoo hung around for about a week, then one night, he jumped out of his goldfish bowl. He was found dried up on the living room floor the next day.

Young Emily was sad to hear the news of her loss but the resiliency of youth soon prevailed. The opportunity to preside over a solemn funeral for Whackadoo, with her whole family in attendance, was adequate consolation and her goldfish was soon forgotten.

Tim did not have a strong opinion on the subject of household pets either way. If Emily would have wanted a dog or cat, he would have been willing to get one. Since she really did not care for indoor pets, he was quite content with chickens, and quite content with his life in general.

He told Emily once that she, "Looked right out of a Norman Rockwell painting," as she returned, barefoot, calico print dress, ponytail, from the nesting boxes with a basket of eggs.

Well, before this little digression, I was informing you of Emily's dinner preparations.

During dinner, Tim declared that the Chicken Of The Woods mushroom was both uncommon and mighty tasty, a compliment which cannot be eclipsed by any other of the culinary variety. As Emily poured Tim a glass of wine, she said, "We have cause to celebrate and I wonder, now that you are 28 years old, my dear Timothy, whether or not you have retained your 'cool' status, the chief attribute of that status being, I was once informed, the ability to infer." She was filling her own glass with what was obviously grape juice as she finished saying that and then she raised her glass for a toast. Tim was staring at her with a wide, open-mouthed half smile. He was still cool.

The next day, Emily and Tim picked up Tricia. The three of them were going up the road to Interstate State Park. "Tim has some exciting news to share with you, would you care to hazard a guess?" said Emily after Tricia got settled into her seat. "No, and don't use that word when we're driving," responded Tricia.

Tim seemed surprised that Emily would have him bestow the glad tidings upon his sister-in-law. He calculated that by responding this way, "Yes, we have achieved successful fertilization," Emily would have the opportunity to make the announcement by way of clarification. He was right. Tricia was thinking gardening all the way. "So, you harvested turnips and put a crate in your root cellar or what? Oh wait, are you incubating chicken eggs?" Emily was shaking her head, "It's me. I'm with child!"

Tricia's face exploded into rapture. Her fists flew into a series of short upper cuts before high fiving Emily and patting Tim on the shoulder saying, "Way to go old chap." Tim felt his face get hot for some reason. His cheeks were as red as a Cortland apple. He was glad Tricia could not see him blush. "When's the due date? Do you know if it's a boy or girl? Have you picked out a name? Why is your face all red Tim?" Tricia's excitement knew no bounds.

Stillwater is situated on the west bank of the St Croix River. Just up the river, at Taylors Falls on the Minnesota side, and St Croix Falls on the Wisconsin side, is Interstate State Park, home to some of the largest glacial potholes in the world.

Just outside Taylors Falls, they passed an open field that looked like it was possibly a thin layer of soil covering an immense loadstone that had, by means of magnetic force, vacuumed several dozen articles of space debris out of orbit.

They saw strange looking metal structures towering above the prairie, a house, or a room at least, was suspended from a steel frame, a jungle gym made out of PVC pipe, a large dome made out of small wooden blocks. Intrigued, Tim pulled into the parking lot of the Franconia Sculpture Park.

As they walked around, Tricia was heard to say, "This is the weirdest place I've ever seen." That was saying a lot, considering some of the house parties she had been to. Emily was particularly interested in reading the artist statements. Some of the statements seemed to be cast with the same degree of randomness as the sculptures. Much of it was as incomprehensible to her as poetry, but she was amused nonetheless. "It does not signify," she said out loud, having read one artist's description of his work and now examining the piece. "It does," countered Tricia, who was looking at it from another angle.

Emily was about to object when someone caught her eye. He was walking with a purpose not ten yards from where they were standing and after a confirming stare, Emily exclaimed, "Benteen? Benteen Willis! Hello, it's Emily and Trish from the Hideaway Resort in Chippewa Falls a couple years ago." Benteen stopped in his tracks and answered, "Greetings, fellow art lovers. How have you been? Did you and that young man ever get married?" (Tim and Emily had shared the happy news, of their engagement, with everyone before they left the resort that week, two years ago.)

Tricia answered, "They not only got married, but Emily's got a bun in the oven!" "You don't say! Well congratulations, I'm very happy for the both of you. Margaret is here somewhere, she would love to see you guys. I'm puttin' together a big solar system sort of thing over there where those cranes are." "Are you exhibiting here?" asked Emily excitedly. "Yep, that's right," said Benteen proudly, "actually, I have some people waiting for me. They are going to help connect two large pieces together. Would you like to see my work?" "We'd love to see it. We'll just collect my husband, who has wandered off somewhere, and meet you over there."

Emily and Tricia found Tim standing at the base of a 25 foot tall, kinetic, steel structure, to which had been mounted a hand crank. Tim had traced the crank mechanism up through the sculpture, and concluded that by turning it, the whole contraption would be set in motion. But there was one problem. The crank was 8 feet off the ground.

"You'll never guess who we just ran into," said Emily as they approached Tim, and after a brief pause, the duration of which was not filled by a response from him, she continued, "well, guess." "You said I would never," said Tim, somewhat distractedly. He was still pondering the elevation of the hand crank. Tricia nodded sympathetically, "You did."

Emily's posture and facial expression made it clear that she was not moving until she received a guess from Tim. This new sculpture that had taken root near him proved to be much more fascinating than the cold steel one that he had been focused on.

With due consideration given to the strange surroundings, Tim ventured his first guess, "Veruca Salt?" "Nope," came Emily's abbreviated response. "Morticia Adams?" Emily shook her head. "The March Hare? Charlie-in-the box?" "It's someone we met at the Hideaway," hinted Tricia, in order to speed the process along. "You saw Farkus here?" "It's Benteen Willis! He's here with an exhibit and Margaret too, though we haven't seen her yet."

Benteen was up on a scaffold, welding two sections of his sculpture together, when the three made it over to the work area. The lower section rested on the surface of planet earth while the upper section was suspended from a trolley mounted chain hoist that could be rolled along an I-beam supported by steel A frames.

Emily thought that the bottom looked like a combination of the Eiffel Tower, a lighthouse, and an astronomer's observatory. The top looked like a model of an atom or maybe a solar system. She recognized some of the parts that Benteen had used, a transmission housing, a couple of mufflers, intake manifold, electric motor, cylinder head, flywheel and so on, all welded or fastened together with other unrecognizable scrap metal to form an eclectic masterpiece.

Margaret greeted them and then explained, "Those top pieces all rotate around each other. He built four sections at the shop back home and is assembling them together here."

The four of them chatted there, under the shower of sparks from Benteen's stick welder, until he was done. "That's all I can do for now. I'll have to wait until the wind dies down to add the next section," said Benteen after climbing down to earth. "Can I read your artist statement?" asked Emily. Benteen looked uneasy, like a child caught with his hand in the cookie jar, "Well, you see, I'm not exactly an artist like these others. Someone in Madison suggested I make something really big to display here and it sounded like fun so Margaret made the arrangements and here I am. I guess I'm not really trying to make a statement." " I could jot down a few ideas," offered Emily. "Sure, if it's not too much trouble mind you," replied Benteen hopefully. Tricia suggested that they have lunch at the park and so they all made their way to a picnic table while Tim was sent to fetch the cooler.

Margaret procured a pen and notebook for Emily. She scratched out the following artist statement for Benteen:

Benteen Willis
Madison, WI

Artist Statement:
My work explores the mystery of continuity. I employ perceptual shifts in depth and curvilinear contours with integrated subtleties to create a point of access to the infinite cascade of universes that are the necessary and inevitable result of the synthesis of mind and

time. I hope to provide an alternative to the temporal, an experience of the transcendent, the sublime, pure simplicity.

Each component of this sculpture has been processed, assembled, employed, discarded, recovered and given a new purpose. The transient nature of material objects, their disintegration and reformation is presented here to demonstrate the incongruity between utility and futility.

Emily slid the notebook, rather sheepishly, over to Benteen when she was done, saying, "It's rather silly." Benteen read it over a few times, shaking his head affirmatively and muttering to himself, then looked up and declared, "I don't understand a word of it. It's perfect!"

Benteen then proceeded to, carefully tear the paper free from the notebook, fold it neatly, and deposit it in the pocket of his flannel shirt. These proceedings were executed with the solemnity of a religious ceremony, and during the ensuing conversation, Emily noticed Benteen's hand venture reassuringly to the pocket more than once. Emily felt pleased to be able to help Benteen. He was a character dear to her heart.

Noticing that the earth had not ceased to spin all the while they had been at their detour, Tim, Emily, and Tricia parted company amicably with Benteen and Margaret, then drove into Interstate State Park.

They visited both sides of the river, hiked the trails, enjoyed the breathtaking views, and examined the rock formations.

With the ink still drying on her recent effort, seemingly successful, Emily felt inspired to pen an artist statement for one of the glacial potholes. She found a pencil in the car and on a napkin, wrote the following.

Artist Statement:
I have named this sculpture: Patience. I use rocks called grinders
and by imparting circular motion to these by the force of moving
water, I was able to form the large bowl shaped cavity you see
here.

My goal was to create a lasting testimony and silent witness to the
power of perseverance. Is this too much? It is not too much. Those
faithful ones who move mountains, one pail at a time, will glory in
the achievement. Be still, gaze at the wonder before you, and
remember, if they ask you; "What is the sign of the Father in you?"
tell them, it is movement and repose.

She left the napkin under a rock near the formation and
hustled off to catch up with Tim and Tricia who were walking a
trail back toward the car.

At one point, they stopped to see what was causing a
commotion in the top of a tall red pine. The pine was growing at
the crest of a hill. Three young eagles were identified and during
the skirmish, an object dropped from the treetop to the trail
ahead of them. They walked up to see what had fallen.

Another party, a couple, had also been watching the
eagles, (At least one of them had been anyway) from the trail on
the other side of the hill, and were walking up to see what had
fallen. Both parties arrived at the dead fish at about the same
time.

"Broglie? Clarinda?" questioned Tricia with surprise. She
accepted their startled reaction as confirmation of her guess.
"I'm Tricia. We met at the Hideaway Resort in Chippewa Falls a
couple of years ago. This day is starting to feel like a Twilight
Zone episode. Earlier today, we ran into Benteen and Margaret,
now you guys, how have you been?"

A brief period of conversation followed in which
everyone became made aware of the recent goings on of the
others. Having dispensed with these pleasantries, the
conversation stalled, leaving silence, the awkwardness of which
138

was felt most acutely by Emily. "Tim missed out on your scientific theory. Are you still working out details on that?" "Oh yes, still working out the details," answered Broglie. The conversation fell silent again.

Realizing that; standing around a dead fish, on a trail in the middle of the woods, at Interstate State Park, was an unlikely venue for a dissertation on theoretical physics, Emily cast about for an exit strategy.

"Have you been to Franconia Sculpture Park? That's where we met Benteen Willis. He's exhibiting there." "Is it far from here?" "No, not at all."

Directions were given and they parted company with best wishes all around. When they were out of earshot, Emily declared, "If I meet up with that little girl Lydia before the end of the day, I'll drop over dead from astonishment."

After a couple of months, Emily quit working at the nursing home to spend more time preparing for the baby. She asked Tricia over frequently to assist with various nesting projects. Tricia responded to these invitations with alacrity for she was practically more excited about the baby than Emily and felt honored to be a part of the preparations.

Tricia was now living in Minneapolis and had one semester of cinematography school remaining, plus an internship, to earn her Associate's Degree. She had lived with her Aunt and Uncle for a year and then had gotten an apartment closer to school. Emily thought her roommate, Amy, was a bad influence on her.

Amy grew up in Stillwater, and was living at home, and attending the same school as Tricia, when they met. They shared rides for most of the first year and then decided to get an apartment. She was 21 years old and eager to experience the nightlife in the Twin Cities.

"It smells like Aunt Portia's bread in here," said Tricia, as she entered Emily's house. "Would you like to try some?" responded her host. "Maybe later, let's get some painting done first."

The two sisters were going to paint the baby room with a fresh white coat of semi-gloss. Emily planned to texture and paint an accent wall either pink or blue once the baby's gender was known.

Lorraine had made some curtains with earth tones and some splashes of yellow. She said they would go with either pink or blue but Emily was not so sure. "What is your opinion of these?" inquired Emily. "They're nice. Did mom make them?" "She did, and oh! She said she could come and stay with us for a couple weeks when the baby is born. That is a great comfort. I'm getting a little nervous." "What about? You've taken care of babies before." "It's not that. I just thought if something goes wrong, it will be nice to know she's here. Tim can't get much time off and you have school." "What do you mean, 'If something goes wrong' what would go wrong?" Emily did not answer right away, but instead starting painting.

Tricia knew, from experience, to be patient while her sister deliberated over how and to what degree she would confer on her some inner confidence. After painting for a while, Emily casually said, "It's probably nothing. Of course I've never been pregnant before so how would I know? But, I feel something isn't right." "Have you asked your doctor about it?" "No, but I might mention it at my next appointment." "Does Tim know?" "I haven't mentioned it to him yet. He's so excited about the baby-" Emily's voice trailed off as if she was going to say more but reconsidered.

Tricia would reflect on this conversation many times in the years to come and wonder if there was anything she could have said or done to change the course of events that time had transformed into memories.

The two continued to paint for some time until Tricia broke the silence, "I think Tim will be a great father. How many grand kids do you guys plan to knock out for old man Vincy anyway?" "Tim said he would welcome a large family but I'm not thinking ahead too much," answered Emily laughing at the remembrance of a comment her father-in-law had made to Tim before they were married and the fact that her sister never forgot things of that nature.

"I wish Tim had a twin brother for me to marry," said Tricia in a general way and without any special feeling. Emily stopped abruptly and looked at her in such a way that a casual observer might have supposed that Tricia's hair had burst into flame while she was talking. As Emily was giving full consideration to Tricia's comment, treating it as a revelation, analyzing its implications and possibilities, Tricia grew impatient and added, "He doesn't have any twin brothers he's been hiding all these years does he?" Emily responded with a sigh, "No twin brothers I am sure, but knowing his father, you may uncover a half brother in some future installment of your night prowlings."

Emily was looking at a thin, fading scar on Tricia's right hand, a reminder that her sister liked to take an occasional walk on the wild side. About one year before this present time, in which we find these two sisters painting a baby room, Tricia, with her brain marinated in Mickey's Malt Liquor and Lime Vodka Sour, had gotten angry about who knows what outside a bar in St Paul and punched a wall, breaking a bone in her hand. The broken bone required a small metal plate and four screws to hold it in place while they fused back together. This plate had been removed about three months ago and only the scar remained.

Tricia's nocturnal habits were an ongoing source of apprehension for the Brooke family. Their appeals to quit drinking would inevitably be overruled by her restless nature and her illusion of invincibility.

There are events in life, a traumatic experience, the loss of a loved one, a brush with death, a crisis or hardship of some sort, which can cause us to reevaluate our priorities, to take our life in a new direction, and look back at the event as a turning point.

Let me lay it all out for you. It was Friday night. Emily was home alone. Tim was out of town, which his job occasionally required of him and Emily was getting ready for bed when the phone rang. Her face blanched when she answered it. "Hello Emily? It's Amy... Tricia's in trouble. She's acting really weird, like, I never seen her this way before... I think someone put something in her drink."

Amy thoroughly admired Tricia and wanted to be seen with her. She thought Tricia looked like a model, enjoyed her sense of humor, and, being four years younger, was deeply impressed by her confidence and experience.

They had gone to a house party, in Stillwater, hosted by one of Amy's old high school friends. Amy had clung, fortunately, to Tricia most of the night, partly because Tricia didn't know anyone else there, (which was never a problem for Tricia) and partly because she wanted to be elevated in the eyes of her old friends by her new association.

Tricia, despite being often over indulgent on such occasions, was always able to retain a thread of inhibition to safeguard her. Tonight, something was disturbingly different, and Amy noticed.

One minute, Tricia was her usual dancing, rowdy self, the life of the party and the center of attention, and then she wasn't. Amy found her quietly sitting on a sofa. The mischievous gleam in her eye had been replaced by a despondent, dull stare. When Amy asked her what was wrong, she responded incoherently and with slurred speech. That's when she called Emily.

Amy wasn't the only one clinging to Tricia that night. Of the two dozen or so partygoers and assorted hangers-on in attendance that evening, there were only a few that Amy didn't recognize. One of those had been hanging around Tricia most of the night and Amy had observed him bring Tricia a mixed drink from the kitchen. Shortly after that, she had started acting strangely. Despite her relative immaturity, Amy had formulated the theory that he had drugged her and regarded her vulnerable state with ill intent.

After securing the address from Amy, Emily quickly regained her composure and got dressed. Fifteen minutes later, she was at the house inquiring after her sister and was led to the bathroom where Amy had sought refuge with her friend.

142

Tricia was unconscious by this time. "There's a guy out there that wanted Trish to leave with him," said a frightened Amy as she closed the bathroom door behind Emily. Emily brushed off her annoyance that Amy had referred to her sister as "Trish" and asked, "What guy? Who is he?" "I don't know who he is. He just sort of showed up here. He had Trish by the arm and was taking her out. She's not herself, she was just like whatever, and was going with him so I made like she whispered something to me and told him that she wanted to go to the bathroom first," answered Amy excitedly as Emily checked her sister's pulse and breathing. Then, having roused Tricia somewhat with gentle shaking, Emily deliberated about whether or not to call for help. She had significant first aid training through her part time work at nursing homes and decided that her own care, and close observation, might spare her sister all the trouble that could arise from a trip to the hospital in an ambulance.

"Let's get her out of here," she urged Amy, and the two of them, each supporting Tricia by her arms, led her out of the bathroom. Emily had underestimated the sinister nature of the situation.

As they were leading Tricia out of the house, they were stopped by the young man who had been hanging around her all night. He was superficially handsome, dark hair, shining white teeth, well formed features, but with a waxen complexion and a faint scar which ran from the corner of his mouth at a downward angle to betray the irony of his smile.

His face was like the façade of an old building that had been painted over and dressed up with new curtains, to obscure dilapidated interior walls, perforated with verminous infestation, mold, and decay. This building's plumbing leaked with a monotonous drip and its inadequate wiring glowed red when the circuits were over taxed. Emily was about to plug a high watt halogen light into this circuitry and was unaware that the fuses had been circumvented.

Smiling and friendly, he approached the three girls and said, "I'll take her home." Emily responded curtly, "You most certainly will not." There was a grave, forbidding, expression

143

that flashed across his face and was gone like a tremor, as if someone in that old dilapidated building had pulled a curtain aside, to see what sort of star was illuminating his comfortable darkness, and then quickly closed the curtain again. "Look, she said I should bring her home. It's ok, we're old friends," came his second friendly attempt. "She's coming home with me. I'm her sister," countered Emily steadfastly. At this, his smile faded slowly away as he looked from Emily to Tricia and back to Emily. Then, he abruptly shrugged his shoulders and turned and started to walk away.

They had made a few steps of progress toward the door when the man suddenly turned around, this time he had a switchblade knife in his hand and the façade wall had crumbled away. He spoke in a barely audible whisper, "I'm taking her," as he reached out to grab Tricia's arm.

Emily grabbed his arm, intercepting his reach for Tricia, and took hold of his other wrist firmly, the knife just inches from her own wrist. Her strength was no match for him. It was her glare, honed sharper than any steel, that held him fast, not her arms, as she said, "We called the police while we were in the bathroom. They'll be here any minute. If you leave now, there won't be any trouble."

He responded with a string of choice words and threats but she did not back down. As he was carrying on this way, Emily cast an imploring glance at two male bystanders who were loitering, wide eyed, nearby. Her look seemed to rouse one of them because he said persuasively, "Yeah man, you should probably go. It ain't worth going to jail."

The man freed his hand from Emily's grasp with a quick, savage movement and turned to leave. At the door, he turned to look back at Tricia but Emily had followed him, keeping herself between him and her, and with her right hand on his shoulder, her left fist clenched and held tight against her waist, she said, "Please just go before the police arrive." As soon as she had backed him out the door, she closed and locked it. Then, turning to Amy she said gravely, "Call the police."

144

Amy's trembling voice had just finished repeating the address to the emergency dispatcher when she suddenly screamed, "Oh my God!" and dropped the phone. Blood was dripping from Emily's left hand into a pool that had collected on the floor at her feet. Her face was pale as she looked in the general direction of Amy but her eyes were focused on nothing in particular.

The blade of the man's knife had cut a deep gash in the palm of Emily's hand as he wrestled his wrist free from her grip.

Amy grabbed a towel and wrapped it around her hand. Others sprang into action and soon the two sisters were sitting on the sofa recovering, one, semi-conscious and drooling, the other, three months pregnant and with a blood soaked towel wrapped around her hand.

As Emily looked about the room blankly, she said, "If mom could see us right now, she'd have a heart attack."

Amy, Tricia, and Emily spent the night at Uncle Henry and Aunt Portia's house. Tricia was absolutely crushed when she was made aware, the next day, of all that had transpired at the house party. In fact, Emily was a bit alarmed at how inconsolably grieved she was.

Tricia slept until early afternoon and when she awoke, she felt tolerably well but could recall nothing from the previous night. Amy told her what happened. At first, Tricia listened with a smug look on her face, seemingly amused by the thought of her feigned whisper and their subsequent sanctuary in the bathroom. But when Amy told her that she had called Emily, Tricia turned pale. When Amy told her about the knife, Tricia's body tensed into a tight knot. When Amy told her about the pool of blood, Tricia looked over to where Emily was sitting, and seeing for the first time, the bandaged hand, she fell into a crumpled pile at Emily's feet and wept bitterly.

Emily pulled her sister up close to her, wiped away her tears, and listened patiently as Tricia swore, remorsefully, that she would never drink again. And do you know what? She never did.

If you are in doubt, dear reader, consider that the characters in this fictional novel, including Tricia of course, are a construct of the author's mind, and further considering that her future exists in my anticipation, you may accept on my authority, that she quit for good.

Tricia simply split the world into two groups of people, drinkers and nondrinkers, and, being strong willed, stepped firmly into the other camp and stayed there.

Did I tell you about the fellow at Harold's foundry that would pick up cigarette butts from the floor and smoke them in his pipe? Not sure why I just thought of that. Anyway, for Tricia, it was just a matter of deciding and then acting as if there was no other way. That's just how her mind worked I guess.

There were times when she longed for a return to her former ways. At these times, she would think of Emily and the longing would subside. Or, if she was feeling a particular urge, she might pay a visit to her sister, and seeing the scar on Emily's hand, she would extinguish any glowing ember of temptation that had flared up.

To fill the void formed by her self-imposed prohibition, Tricia focused all of her energy on her studies.

Chapter 10 Tricia

In the days and weeks following the infamous house party incident, and driven, in part, by guilt, Tricia immersed herself in schoolwork. Books that she had previously skimmed through, cramming the highlights into her short-term memory, just to pass an exam, she now reread from cover to cover, absorbing every detail.

Tricia also began an internship with a company that rented film production related equipment. She was learning on the job, at school, and filling her free time with more study. She became particularly interested in directing and producing video.

Tricia had learned at a young age that possessing physical beauty was conducive to developing an ability to inspire and motivate people to action and she had no reservations about using her own enchantments for that purpose. On the contrary, she had honed her skill to an art form.

Her canvas was the human will. A penetrating stare, a mysterious smile, an accentuating posture, an array of gestures, and the ability to endure an uncomfortable silence without feeling uncomfortable, were lifted from her palette with a brush of abiding confidence. Much of the restlessness that she had felt all her life, however, was related to a feeling that her energy and skill was not being applied to some sublime and meaningful purpose.

With the full purchase of her resources now directed toward cinematography, an idea, one she had previously pursued apathetically, came into clear focus. It was a short film that would fulfill a class requirement, but more importantly, it would be expressive of a sentiment that she had and an outlet to transduce her potential energy into a more kinetic form.

First, Tricia asked her Uncle Henry if he would check into the possibility of her crew doing some filming at the machine shop where he worked. After receiving a positive response, she approached Emily about help with writing a script.

"Of course, I'd love to help. What is the outline of the story?" replied Emily enthusiastically. Tricia unraveled her plan, "Well, the main character is a middle aged man, married with a couple of kids. I have permission to do some filming at Uncle Henry's shop so I made him a machinist."

"Here is a really rough outline of the main scenes." Below is a reproduction of the sheet of paper that Tricia handed to Emily:

148

Scene 1   *A farmer is dropping off a worn out part at the machine shop- says he's trying to keep an older implement going, can't afford a new one and can't get parts for the old one- hopes to get back in the field as soon as possible*

Scene 2   *The main character is driving to work. He stops at a stop sign near a farm field-pauses and looks intently at the field*

Scene 3   *The main character gets to work, at the machine shop, is assigned to repair the worn part that the farmer had brought in earlier, and works overtime to finish it (This will actually involve several scenes but all at the same location)*

Scene 4   *Later that night, main character is home, talking with his wife. He is depressed and feeling like his life is not making a difference- sees an emergency rescue on the evening news*

Scene 5   *In bed that night, the main character has a dream, which will involve several brief scenes, all in the context of the dream- he dreams that a farmer is seriously injured trying to work on his equipment that has a worn part like the one he repaired- emergency vehicles etc.*

Scene 6   *The main character is driving to work, stops at the same stop sign as in scene 2- sees a tractor pulling an old implement in the field*

Scene 7   *A close up shot of the part that the main character had repaired, now installed on the implement and functional*

Emily read the outline carefully while Tricia tried to read her sister's eyes for a clue as to what she thought of it. Her opinion was not discernible in her facial expression, a disconcerting circumstance for someone with an inaptitude for tolerating delay of that sort. Tricia had, at various times in her life, attempted to develop the virtue of patience but always seemed to lack the forbearance to stick with her plan.

"Does the main character realize that the part he repaired was for the tractor implement that he sees when he stops on the way to work?" asked Emily for clarification. "No, he has no idea. He is still depressed in the end," said Tricia. "So he would have to watch the film to know how much impact his work can have on the lives of others and the dream he had was a possible scenario had he not made the repair for the farmer?" questioned Emily, just to be sure she understood. "Exactly," affirmed Tricia with an anxious look.

"I like it. I think the dialogue in scene 4 will be the most critical. It seems to me that your message could be made perfectly clear by the dialogue in that scene," said Emily with enough conviction to relieve Tricia's anxiety.

"We could talk to Steve, he rents our 30 acres, about using his equipment for the final scenes and for advice in general," added Emily. She was convinced that idleness would lead to perdition, in the archaic sense, and if this film project gave her sister something productive to focus on, then she would offer her support without reservation.

Emily's natural curiosity also factored into her enthusiasm. The prospect of a cinematography project opened a broad vista of learning opportunity to her active mind and writing a script would be a stimulating challenge.

Tricia formed her team, which included Amy and three other students. They would work together and all get credit for the project. Tricia assumed the role of producer and director. She asked Amy because she was a friend, but also because she knew a lot of people. Amy would assist with the production and the other three, Brice, Nick, and Mallory, who were more interested in the technical aspects of cinematography, would work on sound, lighting, filming, and editing.

At their first meeting, Tricia's energy was infectious. Everyone wanted to go above and beyond the class requirement. As a result, the technical minds suggested that they rent some equipment rather than use the older stuff from school. They ordered up a Sony Super35 Camcorder and an AJA Ki Pro Mini Recorder along with an assortment of Zeiss lenses, fluid head tripod, LED light kit, stands, and other miscellaneous apparatus. The quote for a three day rental came in at just over $1000 and that was with Tricia's employee discount.

Tricia called Amy after receiving the quote. "Amy, it's Trish, I just got the price on renting the camera and everything. It's over $1000." "How much over?" asked Amy. " "Well, just over. Like, $1050 or something. It doesn't matter, we don't have that much money available. Do you have any ideas?" "We could do a car wash fundraiser in the parking lot of the grocery store!" "It's the middle of winter," Tricia reminded Amy. "Oh, ya," remembered Amy. "Why don't you ask Emily if she has any ideas?"

Tricia was hesitant to call Emily. She had borrowed money from her a few times over the years, and always paid her back, but she always felt that Emily disapproved of how she handled her finances. The last incident involved some concert tickets purchased with money that was needed for her rent payment. This was a different situation, but still, it involved money.

Tricia did call Emily and casually mentioned the rental fee. Emily knew why Tricia had called and casually mentioned that she would ask Tim if he had any ideas. He suggested that Tricia ask the machine shop plant manager if they needed any video produced for advertising or training purposes, and if so, would they pick up the equipment rental fee in exchange for video production.

The suggestion proved to be a brilliant one. The plant manger agreed to the terms and the problem of financing the project was solved.

It was now late January. Winter was beginning to lose its magic for Emily. She was encouraged, however, by the lengthening days and the arrival of seed catalogues in the mail, both a sure sign that spring was still inevitable.

Later that afternoon, the snow drifted down lazily in large flakes and was accumulating significantly on the sidewalk. Emily was five months pregnant and Tim would have to shovel the snow when he got home because if she attempted to do any strenuous activity, he would get upset with her. "You need to rest up and take care of yourself. I can do that," she imagined him saying if she had attempted to do some shoveling. With this thought in mind, Emily shrugged her shoulders and made a cup of Tulsi, Peppermint and Rose Petal Herbal Tea, sat down with a notebook and three sharp pencils, and began writing ideas for the script. She reread Tricia's notes and then proceeded to round the sharp point off the first pencil.

Wife, placing a plate in front of her husband: "What's wrong? You seem quiet tonight." Husband, eating his dinner, reheated from the microwave: "Just tired I guess." Wife, smiling and with encouraging tone: "If you keep working overtime like that, we'll have our house paid off two years early."

A sharp pain, that almost took her breath away, interrupted her writing for a moment. This was a familiar pain that had been gradually increasing in intensity and she would have attributed it to her pregnancy except that she had first noticed it, in a much milder form, before she conceived. Eventually, the pain subsided, which led Emily, whose tendency was to put a positive spin on everything, to believe that these occasional spells were not indicative of a serious condition. She was also aware of a more constant feeling that something just wasn't quite right but did not consider that the two sensations were related.

After finishing her tea, she made a phone call to Steve, and having secured some particulars from him, she set her pencil in motion again.

Wife, sitting down at the table: "What were you working on today?" Husband, dejectedly: "Had to repair a driveshaft for some sort of farm implement." / -Trish, could one of his children, maybe about nine years old, come into the kitchen at this point and ask for help with a school project?/ "Dad, I need your help. Next week we are having career day at school and I need to make a poster board about your job. I want to put on there how your work helps other people, like, farmers grow food to feed people and doctors cure diseases and stuff like that." Husband: "Well, most of the parts I make at the shop are components that get assembled into machinery or equipment that is used in factories or processing plants. They make products that become part of something else. Eventually, somebody buys the end product and is helped by it I guess." Wife: "Just today you fixed that drive something or other," Husband: "Driveshaft." Wife: "Driveshaft, for a farmer. So in a way, you are feeding people indirectly."

Emily discovered that script writing was not as easy as she imagined. She decided to forge ahead, not really satisfied with her effort, but thinking, "It's just a rough draft so I can see if Trish thinks I'm on the right track."

Husband: With resignation and a hint of sarcasm, "I sometimes help feed people indirectly. Is there room on your poster board to put that?" Wife: "Your father has had a long day. I'll help you get started and we'll ask him if we have a question."

Mrs. Vincy, noticing the time and that her husband would soon return home from work, finished with a flourish, wrote a note to Tricia, sealed the papers in an envelope addressed to her sister, and placed it in the mailbox, as she was not likely to see her in the next few days.

Emily was not ignorant of the modern technological forms of communication at her disposal. She just had a nostalgic

153

feeling about letter writing and especially liked to receive letters in the mail. It was her contention that certain inferences could be drawn from reading a hand written letter as opposed to one generated by a keyboard. She would notice if the pen or pencil had been pressed down particularly hard on a certain word or if the penmanship seemed hurried or relaxed. If a word was crossed out or erased, she would try to figure out what the author considered unworthy of publication.

A letter was a tangible object that the originator had physically touched. Sometimes, there were smudges or odors on the paper that became additional clues to decipher. Emily had been sure to spritz a little of her best perfume on all the letters that she had sent to Tim. She thought letter writing was quaint, romantic, and it reminded her of life in a slower paced era, an era that she had only experienced through classic literature.

Vaguely imagining that Tim would return home from work in the same state of melancholy as the husband in her script, Emily planned to meet him at the door with a kiss and dote on him that evening with reassuring attentions.

When Tim did arrive home however, he was in a particularly good frame of mind. He had been notified of a salary increase and suggested that they go out for dinner to celebrate.

At dinner, Emily confided her troubles to Tim, not her pain, but her trouble with writing the script. He suggested that Emily visit the machine shop where the filming would take place. This suggestion was met with approbation. The next day, Emily joined Tricia and the film crew.

Emily was fascinated by the machine shop. Her attention was immediately drawn to an old, battleship grey, Kearney and Trecker horizontal milling machine that was roughing out a large slab of steel. The metal chips coming off the cutter hit the floor with a sound that made her think someone was dropping fifty-cent pieces. The mill was built during World War II by order of the War Production Board and was still operating today, a blend of cast iron, gears, and electricity that harmonized like poetry. It filled her senses like a physical manifestation of a piece of classical music.

By the time of Emily's visit, Tricia had charmed the entire crew and had free reign in the shop. Tricia and her accomplices had a great respect for the workers and their work and they were very careful not to interrupt production or get in the way. They were keenly aware of the potential for accident and observed every safety precaution, which earned them the trust of the employees on the floor and the management. Henry and his coworkers enjoyed the novelty of young fresh faces and were genuinely interested in the filming process. Machinists are, in general, a curious lot.

Emily watched an engine lathe turn the diameter of a shaft. At first, she thought the machinist was manufacturing springs. Then she realized that the spring-like chips were excess steel that was being cut away. Flood coolant was being applied to the cutting tool, which made it difficult to see the cutting action in detail.

After some time had passed, the old fellow that was running the lathe turned to Emily and asked if she would like to try her hand at operating the machine. Emily declined at first, intimidated by the array of levers and switches, but the old gentlemen seemed a little disappointed so she agreed to give it a go as long as he would stay close by.

He gave a rudimentary explanation of what was going on, some brief instructions as to how to operate the lathe, and even showed her how to read a micrometer.

Emily took a deep breath and engaged the lever that set the carriage in motion. She followed the progress of the cutting tool with nervous attention. Her instructions were to disengage the feed lever when the tool reached a groove that had been cut as a stress relief area. If this was not done quickly, the tool would crash into a shoulder and likely spoil the whole part.

Having stopped the carriage movement without incident, Emily turned to ask whether she should turn the feed wheel clockwise or anticlockwise to back the tool out, she couldn't remember which way, but her mentor was nowhere to be seen. "So much for staying close by," muttered Emily.

Then she noticed Tricia and her crew approaching. Not wishing to appear abandoned, Emily decided to try clockwise, with caution. This caused the tool to advance into the shaft and when she stopped, the tool rubbed and chattered on the part so she quickly turned the wheel counter clockwise and then stopped the spindle rotation by pushing yet another lever down. This was accomplished just as Tricia reached the area.

"Look at you, machining up a storm over here," said Tricia with amusement. "Yes, I thought I might as well make myself useful as long as I was hanging about," replied Emily as if she actually knew what she was doing, "Hand me over that micrometer will you?" Tricia handed her the micrometer without having to ask what a micrometer was. "Don't drop it whatever you do."

Emily measured her part carefully. "One and two hundred eighty seven micro inches," she declared after studying the instrument closely. "Micro inches?" questioned Tricia with a doubtful look. Emily knew micro inches didn't sound quite right and realized she had underestimated the degree to which her sister had become familiar with the machining process. She knew her playful deception was exposed. Other than balancing the checkbook, Emily had avoided numbers as much as possible these last couple years. She had not read a Hot Rod magazine since the wedding and 'thousandths' had not been part of her vernacular for a long time.

Filled with pride in her sister, and wishing to acknowledge her superiority in the arena of precision measurement, Emily simply bowed as if she were a civil war era southern gentleman, and, speaking of gentleman, the old one that had left the petite Emily at the controls of a 10 horsepower engine lathe was seen carrying a dusty cardboard box over to an old vertical mill. He motioned the group over.

This mill had not been moved in decades and there were two depressions worn into the concrete floor where the operator most often stood.

From the dusty box was produced a strobe light. Once this was set up, the old fellow adjusted the speed to match the rpm of the spindle so that, instead of a blur, the end mill appeared to be at rest. By varying the speed of the strobe slightly, the end mill appeared to be cutting slowly through the material. The shearing action of the tool's cutting edge could be seen as if rotating in slow motion.

Tricia's crew set up lights and captured video of the process. Coordinating the lighting and camera lenses for the shot took over an hour and Tricia told Emily that they would probably only use a few seconds of the video but it was worth the effort.

Emily's appreciation for the art of cinematography was elevated to a new level, a level whose expanse was also now occupied by her appreciation for the art of metal machining.

As she watched Tricia interacting with the crew she had assembled, and the machine shop workers, she knew her sister had found her niche. "If only she could get settled in a relationship," Emily thought to herself. This thought was still lingering in her mind later on when they had finished for the day and were driving home together. "Brice seems nice," she mentioned casually to Tricia.

Tricia perceived the implications of Emily's rhyme immediately. "Too nice for my taste," she responded definitively. "Perhaps you should reevaluate what attributes you find desirable if you are ever to settle into a serious relationship," stated Emily. She kind of regretting saying it after it had come out but Tricia did not take offense. "I'm not as patient as you. I can't imagine myself molding someone into the character that I want them to be through two years of letter correspondence," said Tricia with resignation. "That's not what happened," replied Emily defensively, then, realizing it kind of was what happened, she added, "Look, we all just want you to be content, but you seem to have a certain animosity toward men. They're either too nice, or too phony, or too tall, or too something. You seem to be focused always on faults."

Tricia didn't answer right away. She did not disagree with Emily's assessment but rather, was searching her past for the source of her aversion. She wanted to meet someone that worked hard like her father, Harold, and was young and interesting. Someone, someone like Tim, but she couldn't tell Emily that.

Emily could read nothing in the expressionless face of her sister while Tricia was contemplating her state of affairs. Brightening, Emily suggested that they stop for coffee. She wanted to pursue the subject that she had introduced but without distracting Tricia from her driving too much.

Emily and Tricia found a cozy booth at a café and as Tricia looked around, she initiated the conversation this way; "This looks like the sort of place Tim's dad would be stopping in at," and then turning toward Emily with a sullen look, she added, "does Tim ever talk about Claire?" Emily looked steadily at her sister and responded calmly, "Not much."

Tricia frowned and sipped her coffee. After a brief silence, Emily said, "Are you feeling depressed?" "Not particularly," shrugged Tricia. They sat like two poker players, reading each other's eyes for a clue.

Then, with an abrupt change of tone, Tricia said, "Sometimes I wish I wasn't so attractive." This comment caught Emily by surprise, as evinced by her quizzical look. "Don't give me that look, you know that all of us Brooke girls are attractive to men. It's not vanity to say it. It's just a fact. Except that for me it may be a curse, not a blessing. I mean, you have Tim and he loves you for who you are, not just your appearance. Liz has Jim and, although he's not exactly my type, he's perfect for Liz." Realizing she had excluded Jim from her ideal and not Tim, Tricia quickly tried to make her point, hoping that Emily would not perceive her omission.

"I can never trust that a guy is really interested in me and not just infatuated by some sort of physical attraction. Sometimes I think that if I was plain, things would be so much easier."

Emily had a deep level of comprehension for words spoken or omitted. It was her gift. She offered the following advice, nothing different than she had offered ten times before,

158

and as such, no more than a place holder in the conversation while she ruminated on Tricia's admission.

"Perhaps if you presented yourself in a more modest fashion, you would attract someone worthy of you." Tricia had tried Emily's suggestion, half-heartedly, a few times, but to no avail.

Emily recalled a conversation that the two of them had, while painting Francesca's room before she was born, whereby Tricia lamented the absence of a brother of Tim for her to marry, a twin brother no less.

Emily cast about for some other topic of conversation to introduce while she thought through Tricia's dilemma. She did not see that a topic of conversation was sauntering over to their booth.

"Howdy ladies. Can I buy you another cup of coffee?" "We were just leav..." started Emily but was drowned out by Tricia who had slid over in her seat. "Have a seat cowboy. She's married and I'm joining a convent, but if you want to spend your money, I'll have another cup."

The man slid his square shoulders into the booth seat and motioned to the waitress. He was wearing an old baseball cap and a plaid western shirt with pearl snaps. His age was hard to guess. He had a confident ease about him that seemed born of experience and the features of a rugged outdoorsman, but there was a youthful tone to his deep voice and a roundness to his face that seemed at odds with his rugged confidence.

"I hope you're not joining just to get away from a man," he said, emphasizing the word 'man', as the waitress filled their coffee cups.

"I hope you're not joining us just to get away from your wife," countered Emily, noticing his wedding ring. "No, I'm happily married, you got that right. No, I just wanted to share some information with you," said the man as he produced a pamphlet from his back pocket.

"I'm with a group that has been studying the state of things in the world for some time now. The thing is, the world, as we know it, is coming to an end. In fact, we are headed toward a

159

cataclysmic disaster. The group that I belong to is establishing a community that will repopulate the earth after the day of reckoning. It's all spelled out in this brochure."

"Where are you setting up shop?" asked Tricia. "Wyoming." "Well, what are you doing here in Minnesota then?"

"Right then. I'll get right to the point. You see, I'm a recruiter. I'm traveling around the country, looking for just the right sort of people, to settle with us. You two ladies look healthy, fertile, and well formed, and would add an upper midwestern element to our genetic pool. There'd have to be DNA testing and background checks, that sort of thing of course."

Emily felt like a piece of meat at the butcher shop that had just been purchased by a discerning carnivore.

"How do we join?" asked Tricia with sarcastic innocence. "What my sister meant to say was, we're not interested thank you." "But if we were," said Tricia, giving her sister a look to check her interference, "how would we find you?" "My number is on the back of this," replied the man as he set the brochure down on the table for the girls to see. "Sons And Daughters of the Never Ending World Settlement," read Emily, "catchy name." "Yes mam. SAD NEWS. And it will be on October 9th, 2019." "That's when it's all going down?" asked Tricia. Nodding gravely, the man said, "That's the date we have calculated. It doesn't give us much time," then looking exclusively at Tricia, "Think about it. I'll be in town for a few more days."

As the man sauntered off, Emily teased, "Are you thinking about it?" "Maybe," replied Tricia with a tone that made Emily uneasy.

Chapter 11   The Premier

Harold and Lorraine drove up from Milwaukee along with Jim, Elizabeth and Liz to attend the premier of Tricia's film. The school had made arrangements with a local theatre to show all of the cinematography projects on the big screen. It was a big event. Big. Sometimes I find that words I use ordinarily, words in common use, seem strange all of a sudden. All of a sudden? Sometimes phrases too.

"Isn't this exciting?" whispered Lorraine as they sat down near the front where Tricia had four seats reserved. Harold nodded and took his wife's hand in his. Elizabeth sat next to Lorraine. Jim had offered to hang near the back with Liz.

Tim was out of town on business, something that could not be postponed because of the nearness of Emily's due date. The fourth seat was occupied by a balding, middle-aged, man. Emily was going to sit elsewhere, rather than confront the man about her seat, but Tricia, who was a few rows ahead, caught her eye and through signs and expressions, made it abundantly clear that Emily was to sit next to Elizabeth.

For Tricia's sake, Emily approached the man, and in the pleasant tone that was natural to her, made the following observation; "Excuse me sir, but I think this seat is reserved, my sister made the arrangements, that's her just up there," pointing to Tricia who was now engaged in other business, "it means a lot to her that I sit with my family," nodding in their direction. Their attention was directed at the aisle where Jim and Liz were still standing.

At first the man made no reply and remained in the seat with his arms crossed and an obstinate look on his face, but eventually he got up in a huff and moved down a few seats, muttering to his associates, "Now I won't be able to see a damn thing thanks to her." His new seat was directly behind a tall women with big hair. BIG hair.

Emily sat down. The seat next to her was occupied by a scowling women, probably in her fifties, who slid her purse across the floor with her foot saying, "I suppose my purse is in your way too." Emily made no reply.

Treading the sticky network of divergent, self-oriented wills, that is an integral aspect of the fallen human condition, would not be so very difficult, excepting that one meets up with the venomous adversary, who moves easily across this web, which is, after all, his own issue, spun in the blackness of his darkness. His whispers are not without their influence. His deception is adapted to time and place. His goal is complete isolation.

Keeping company with such a one is so contrary to our being, that no one would choose it, if it were not for the alluring lie.

A shaft of light connected the screen to an opening in the projector room behind them. Particles of dust floated in this shaft, like tiny fish in a cool, clear stream. Now that the light has illuminated what was otherwise unseen, you have to think about breathing in all those tiny fish. Your eyes cry out, 'return o comfortable darkness' but your lungs are not making a fuss. They can handle a few dust minnows.

Emily was amazed at the clarity and detail of the video. Tricia was able to plug her laptop directly into the digital projector at the theatre and reproduce the video in high definition. The machining process was brought to life with amazing detail, the actors, inexperienced as they were, did an amazing performance, but the derision from the people to Emily's left did not leave off even during the screenings.

Gestures and comments, seen and heard by only her, made her wish the whole thing was over with so that she could get away from them. "It means a lot to her that I sit with my family," said one, with a mock imitation of Emily's voice. "Probably got those at Walmart. Looks anorexic to me. Thinks she owns the place I guess," and so on. But they had unwittingly saved the worst for last, "She probably wrote the stupid script for this one."

Emily absorbed all these comments like a sponge and would not let one drop of this venom touch her family after the film was over.

Elizabeth wanted to compliment Tricia in a special way that would show, her appreciation of Tricia's accomplishment was genuine, but how to do it? She would probably think it was just more obligatory familial verbiage, words that would ring hollow because they came from a sibling.

Her answer came from observing her father, who said nothing to Tricia, but gave her a hug, a tear streaming down his cheek.

Lorraine, who had sat down, trying not to think of all the gum that was probably stuck to the bottom of the seats, became fascinated by the movie, and the idea that her own offspring had produced it. She kept wondering, "How did they do that?" Lorraine's questions were answered by Tricia's crew, at a reception, following the screening.

At the reception, Henry and Harold were exchanging anecdotes from their careers and Tricia was tuned into that conversation. "When I first started in the business, at a shop in Minneapolis, I was mentored by an old timer that had about forty years of experience," Henry was saying. "One day he was indicating in a part in a four jaw chuck and I asked him why he didn't just clamp it in a three jaw scroll chuck. I still remember his answer to this day. He said; 'There are three worthless things in a machine shop. The foreman, the reamer, and the three jaw chuck.' Well, I thought this was sage wisdom until I got hired on at another shop and learned how to use a reamer properly, drill a hole, bore it straight, then finish ream it to size, chucking it on the end of the shank so the tool can find its own way and not reproduce the runout in the collet." Harold was nodding as if he understood perfectly. Tricia asked, "What about the three jaw chuck?" "I also learned about soft jaws for scroll chucks and all the applications for those. The first shop I worked at never used them," answered Henry. "What about the foreman?" asked Harold with a smile. "I found out later that the foreman and my mentor were fishing buddies and always gave each other a hard time," finished Henry.

Tricia could have listened to shop talk all day but felt obliged to make the rounds and thank everyone for coming, and, in the case of Emily, for her help. Emily was dissatisfied with her contribution but made a gracious reply, in order to hide her misery. She missed Tim and found it hard to enjoy the reception, the bitter vileness from the theatre, still fresh in her memory.

Time has a way of healing such wounds, however, and after a week, other activities and memories soon occupied her thoughts and mind. After all, there was a baby to get ready for.

Chapter 12   William Vincy

When you smoke Camel straights, you are as likely as not to get bits of tobacco in your mouth before you are finished with one. Bill Vincy spit his tobacco bit on the floor as he sat at his kitchen table, drinking his morning coffee. After all, what did he care? He had no women in the house to complain about it. Small consolation for the empty feeling of waking up alone everyday, he thought to himself. He spat on the floor again with an ironic grin on his haggard face.

Bill looked ten years older than he actually was. His lifestyle was not conducive to long life or a young countenance. In fact, Bill had slept at least two hours less than he should have, on average, every day, for the last thirty years. That means he would have to sleep for two and a half years straight to get caught up. Not that it would do him any good now.

It was in the morning, while he waited for the caffeine and ibuprofen to erase the pain from his stiff joints and aching muscles, that he had time to reflect on his life. It was in the morning that he missed Clare. It was in the morning that they would have their best conversations, or would not talk at all but just sit and drink coffee and watch the sun come up or watch young Tim at play. Substituting a cup of coffee for an hour of sleep is not a good long term plan, but it had never occurred to Bill that there was any other way. His vices were as essential to him as oxygen.

Bill never had a thought that began with, "If only I had..." He understood that other people lived their lives at a slower pace than he, that some men ate vegetables and didn't drink or smoke, that there were people who were content with little money and few possessions, he understood that, sure he did, but he also understood that fish live underwater and that option was no more available to him than any of those other lifestyles were. He was resigned to his fate.

Staring down through blood shot eyes, Bill saw all his future prospects codified in the symbols before him. A full ashtray, a half empty coffee cup, and an empty chair across the kitchen table from him, were stark reminders of what had become his reality.

When he was feeling particularly low, he might stop by and pay Emily a visit, even if Tim was at work. Emily was an antidote to his gloom. He admired his daughter-in-law, and revered her outlook on life, but with never a thought for conversion. Emily was fond of these visits and enjoyed Bill's company, although he always seemed inaccessible to her somehow.

Bill Vincy did not learn to speak by observing cottagers from a chink in their wall while spending the winter hiding in a hovel attached to the outside of their dwelling. He never uprooted his family, and moved across the country, in an old Hudson, with the prospect of finding work there based on the sole authority of an orange han'bill. Bill never wore rope soled shoes or sought shelter from daisy-cutter splinters in a foxhole, never stored his guineas in an iron pot under the floor beneath his loom. Old Bill had never signed on as a harpooneer with Captain Ahab for the ninetieth lay or lashed a great fish to the side of his boat only to have it ravaged by sharks before he could get back to shore.

But Bill Vincy's exploits were known to Emily and that is how she thought of him, like a literary character whose exploits she had become familiar with, a character whose life was so far removed from her experience that she thought of him almost as though he were fictional.

On this particular morning, Bill was startled by a phone call. It was not unusual for him to get a call at that time of day, or any other time of the day or night for that matter, but the phone seemed to ring with a certain distinction this morning. Something about it's tone or volume or the duration of the rings seemed different, as if it was ringing with more urgency than usual.

Bill answered and then quickly hung up and made a few calls of his own. In a matter of minutes, he had his schedule cleared for the day. He got dressed with great dispatch and left for the hospital; Emily was having her baby.

Tricia and Bill arrived at the hospital at the same time like two children on Christmas morning. The upper cables of the elevator were slack as they rode to the third floor together. Emerging from the confines of their vertical transportation, Tricia and Bill assailed the nurse on duty with excited questions. Having been assured that, "It is going to be a while," Bill proceeded to pace the hallways and Tricia set up broadcast headquarters in a lounge. She contacted everyone she knew, by every conceivable form of communication, and instructed them to stay tuned for big news was imminent.

Several hours later, Emily gave birth to a healthy baby girl. Of the four adults who gazed with wonder on the precious bundle cradled in Emily's arms, it would be difficult, based on appearance, to say which was the most exhausted. Of course, Emily would have the legitimate claim on that title, but she was glowing and did not appear to be anything less than radiant. A soft light, electromagnetic radiation from a fluorescent source in the ceiling, reflected off Tim, Tricia, and Bill and made them visible, but Emily seemed to be illumined by a source from within.

His exhausted aspect notwithstanding, Bill appeared two or perhaps three years younger as he marveled at the little princess that would, from that day forward, exercise dominion over his heart.

Tim and Emily Christened the baby: Francesca, after the Italian saint who had exhibited heroic virtue in the late 1300's.

Francesca's story had made a deep impression on Emily at a young age.

Tim and Emily settled naturally into a new routine as a young family. Tim had no siblings and did not have much experience with babies but he trusted Emily's ability and learned from her. She, with a confidence born of experience, was relaxed enough to maintain a romantic flame in their relationship and support Tim with a comfortable home to return to after work.

Emily was a thrifty household manager and a responsible steward of Tim's paycheck. She made the necessary purchases, paid the bills, and still was able to put a little in their savings account each month.

Tim would sometimes listen smugly as his equal salaried coworkers, whose wives also worked, would complain about having to pick up their child from day care after work, then go home and cook dinner because their spouse was working late that day. From what Tim could gather, these two income households were not even solvent and were building credit card debt.

It was the same story when he got together with his friends that were now married. He felt like a crime scene investigator trying to discover why all their money seemed to disappear each month. Meanwhile, the Vincy estate was prospering under the competent management of his young bride.

Tim had only a vague idea what items such as groceries, clothes, and furniture cost. He had only to toss his paycheck on the desk each week and these necessities appeared by some mysterious process of exchange.

Growing up in the Brooke household, home economics were assimilated by all three Brooke girls, from their mother, Lorraine. Emily made her own laundry soap from Fels-Naptha, Borax, and Arm and Hammer Super Washing Soda. She refinished the top of an old kitchen table that her Aunt Portia had given her and reupholstered an old sofa that she had bought at a garage sale.

Bill had been called upon for assistance with the sofa purchase. Emily had struck the bargain and the sellers agreed to hold it for her. She arranged for Tim to leave her the truck the next day and for her father-in-law to help load.

The sale was still going on the following day when they arrived to pick it up. Bill was immediately drawn to an old mounted fish, a northern pike, and began to haggle over the price, which was only twenty dollars.

He examined the fish, pointing out flaws and scratching his chin doubtfully. This tactic was met with derision from the sellers, however, and so Bill changed his strategy accordingly. He expressed that the price was certainly fair, but if only he wasn't on such a tight budget. Making a deal brought out the competitive side of Bill.

Emily was eavesdropping on the whole proceeding and was compelled to offer mediation but checked herself when the sellers offered to sell the fish for fifteen dollars.

"I'll have to think about it," said Bill as he sidled over to sift through some old record albums. Emily asked if he was looking for anything in particular. "No, not really," he replied, casting a sidelong glance in the direction of his rivals. "Let's get that sofa loaded up."

Bill left empty handed, had Emily drive around the block, then returned with the announcement that he had found some coins in his ash tray, which was not used for it's intended purpose owing to the prohibitive cost of cigarettes, and would they consider an offer of twelve dollars and thirty seven cents?

Whether out of sympathy or just to be rid of Bill, Emily could only guess, but they accepted this offer only to have Bill counter his own offer with the suggestion that a twelve dollar sale price would save them the bother of making change.

Another concession was grudgingly made by the sellers and the deal was finally consummated.

William collected his prize in his arms, beaming with pride as if he had caught the fish himself, and indeed he had, tossed the sellers a twenty-dollar bill and said, "Keep the change."

Bill Vincy had lost his faith. As he got older, he realized the game was rigged and lost his faith. Coming to the realization that the federal government was going to just keep printing money and giving it away, he no longer put his trust in the system. "Do you know what the Federal Reserve is?" he asked Emily on the way home. "Well, not really," replied she. "Not many people do," observed Bill.

"We work long hours to earn notes from the Federal Reserve, trusting that at some future time, we will be able to exchange them for some goods or services that we need or want. It's a faith based system that is going to crash and burn, perhaps in our lifetime."

Emily made no response. Deep in troubled thought, a dark shadow fell across her expression. Ephemeral, it gradually gave way to a more peaceful glow as she remembered that her and Tim were not heavily invested in the sordid scheme.

Bill articulated what Emily was thinking, "You guys will be alright, Tim's handy and you're a shrewd and thrifty homemaker. Yeah, you guys will be alright." Bill smiled, content in the knowledge of his son and daughter-in-law's alrightness.

Emily had made dresses and skirts from quality fabrics that she acquired on sale, and some dress shirts for Tim, but more often she would purchase end of the season bargain clothing items, disregarding the size, for she would custom tailor them to a perfect fit.

Sometimes she would buy a plain dress and trim it out with lace or modify it in some way. When she shopped for clothing, she imagined the potential of each article as if it were a starting point for negotiation rather than a finalized deal.

Her favorite skirt, she had made by cutting six-inch wide strips from several different fabrics. The strips were sewed into rings and the rings sewed one on top of the next with an elastic band on the inside of the top ring. A light pink floral print, a plain white strip cut from an old bed sheet, a candy stripe band, and a raspberry floral from some old curtains were among the treasured pieces incorporated into her masterpiece.

Emily's home, like her wardrobe, was filled with elegant charm. The degree to which Tim appreciated this, dawned on him one day when visiting a friend.

His friend's wife worked outside the home so they had a cleaning lady come in once a week. It was clean, to be sure, sterile might be a better word to describe it, and the rooms were filled with expensive furnishings, but they seemed out of place some how. The furniture seemed to have a gloss to it, almost as if the items were delivered that day and the cellophane packaging had yet to be removed. The carpet still had vacuum cleaner lines in it.

Tim sat uncomfortably on the sofa as he looked around the room, trying to discern precisely what it was that he objected to. The walls were white and sparsely decorated, but with expensive art pieces. When he had been a bachelor, he would have considered this home a model to be strived for, but now he felt that his friend was impoverished in these bleak surroundings.

It came about, in the due course of time, that Tim and Emily were invited out for dinner and drinks by the aforementioned couple, and so, left the baby with Tricia and met them and one other couple.

Emily sat in her homemade pink skirt, like a flower in full bloom, listening intently and with genuine interest while the two other pant suited women talked about how stressful their jobs were and how busy their lives were and then, both looking at Emily, as if suddenly aware that she was not adding to the conversation, asked, "And what do you do?"

Emily, seldom at a loss for words, responded, "Oh, not much compared to the two of you I am sure," but the question set her mind reeling through her day. What had she done? Her days were so varied that it was difficult to recount them in a succinct form.

After seeing Tim off to work and tending to the chickens, she had met a new acquaintance for coffee. Her new friend was also a new mother and they discussed their families, shared decorating ideas and favorite websites, and even engaged in a friendly debate on the forbidden subjects; politics and religion.

On the way home, Emily picked up some groceries and stopped by the hardware store. While Francesca napped, she read (The First Circle, Solzhenitsyn) until her Aunt Portia dropped in for a visit. Emily got out her seed catalogs and asked her Aunt to help plan her garden.

After Aunt Portia left, Emily rewired an old lamp with the aid of a YouTube video and some parts from the hardware store. She was thus engaged when Tim returned home and since they were going out for dinner, she had but to freshen up a bit and get Francesca ready for Tricia.

And so her days went, each day a new adventure as far as she was concerned, with little stress and much amusement.

The two business-women were not satisfied with her evasive answer however, "But *where* do you work?" they persisted. "At home mostly," replied Emily simply. "More companies are allowing employees to work from home, but I don't think I would get much out of my team if I allowed them to work at home," replied one of the women while the other sipped her wine. "No, I agree," said the other, then to Emily, "What *company* do you work for anyway?" "Actually, Tim is the sole source of income at the Vincy household," replied Emily without a hint of embarrassment or shame.

To which one of the women responded in a patronizing tone, "Ohh. Hang in there. You'll find something soon."

Not all was peace and serenity at the Vincy acres. In July, a grey squirrel decided that their attic was the only possible place in which to build a nest and had chewed a hole through the siding near a gable vent.

At first, they tried to scare the squirrel off by tossing pinecones and sticks at it. These efforts proved futile so Tim purchased an extension ladder and nailed some chicken wire over the hole. The squirrel circumvented this discouragement with such apparent ease that Tim and Emily sought the advice of Emily's uncle Henry.

Henry advised that they purchase a small-bore shotgun, adding that he could loan them one, but it would certainly be needed again and so why not invest in one to own?

Tim bought a .410 break action single shot and a box of shells on the way home from work the next day and, having no experience with guns, asked Henry to teach him how to use it safely.

Henry briefly explained the rules of firearm safety and showed Tim how to load and fire the weapon. Emily listened with keen interest, as this was all new to her as well.

Tim dispatched the squirrel and thought that he had put an end to the matter, but the next day, Emily reported hearing a noise in the attic. An investigation followed and to Tim's dismay, the source of the noise was discovered to be a nest full of very young squirrels.

"Now what do I do?" lamented Tim after climbing down from the attic to consult with his wife. "Can't you just shoot them?" wondered Emily. She wouldn't even allow a cat or dog in her house. She certainly was not going to tolerate squirrels in her attic. "I don't want to blow the side of the house out!" exclaimed Tim. Emily was no ballistics expert, but she was pretty sure that their little peacemaker was not capable of serious damage to the house structure.

"I'll do it then," she said firmly, but with no intention whatsoever of going up into that attic. Baby squirrels were cute, but in a dark, confined space? That was just creepy. Her bluff roused Tim's manly courage however. He gathered up the necessary equipment and went back up into the attic without a word.

Emily heard three shots from the .410, some scuffling and scraping, and saw Tim descend the attic ladder with a large bag full of nesting material and dead squirrels. His face was white and drenched with sweat.

Emily rewarded Tim with special attentions for a few days, as if he were a soldier recently returned from battle. After some minor repairs to the gable siding, the incident was over.

Uncle Henry's advice, that a small shotgun would prove to be a valuable tool around the homestead, proved prophetic in an incident that I will now relate.

Tim was out of town for a few days and Emily had undertaken a painting project in the house.

So caught up in her project was she that she had forgotten to lock up the chicken coop until it was after dark. The hens were allowed to range about during the day but would roost at night in the coop where Tim or Emily would lock the door for their safety. A flashlight in hand, she went out to secure her flock. All hens were accounted for so she latched the door and turned to go back inside. She paused half way back to the porch with an odd feeling that something was amiss, but Francesca was in the house so she didn't linger.

Later that night, 2:35 am to be precise, she awoke to a sound like cats fighting and a chicken clucking. Her hens never made any sound at night that she was aware of, so she had no little cause for alarm at hearing one at this time of the night. She went out to investigate, only to discover a raccoon in the chicken coop. At first, she tried to scare it away, thinking that the masked bandit had forced it's way in somehow. This effort was exerted without success however, for reasons that she would learn the next day. "What sort of mischief are you about?" she asked the intruder.

Searching with her flashlight, she saw, at the bottom of the coop, a dead hen, one of her favorites. Emily marched back to the house, in a fury, to arm herself. She reemerged into the dark night a few minutes later, fumbling with the mechanism that would open the action and allow her to load a shell. She opened it, loaded it, and snapped it shut with a satisfying, heavy click.

The raccoon sat motionless on the two by four that was meant for the hens to roost on. He perhaps thought that if he held really still, he could not be seen. Emily pointed the flashlight and the shotgun both at the target, allowed a brief concern that she might, "blow the side of the coop out," pass through her mind and be dismissed, and then squeezed the trigger. Nothing happened. She soon realized that she had forgot to cock the hammer first, an omission that was easily remedied.

A loud crack followed and the raccoon dropped to the floor, kicked its back legs for a few seconds, and then lay as motionless as the dead hen nearby.

"Serves you right," muttered Emily as she ejected the shell from the .410. Then she returned back to the house and was asleep a half hour later.

Emily was half way through her cup of morning coffee the next day before she remembered the deads that she had left lying on the floor of the hen house. After a brief consultation with her Aunt Portia, she went out with a shovel and buried her dead chicken. She then bagged up the dead raccoon and placed it in the chest freezer for her cousin to pick up later in the month. He wanted to tan the hide and make a coonskin cap out of it.

With these chores accomplished, she went back to find the breach in her security, and make any necessary repairs. After circumnavigating the coop for 15 minutes with Francesca, she could not find any point of entry, that could be considered even remotely large enough for a raccoon, such as the one in her freezer, to have used to gain its unwelcome admission.

Emily came to the conclusion that the raccoon must have slipped into the coop just before she went out to lock it up. It must have hid menacingly in the shadows when she came out and got locked in with the chickens. The only mystery remaining was; why did it wait so long to attack a hen? Much speculation has been applied to this question but no definitive answer has been reached.

Later that day, Emily had put everything back in order and was sitting on the living room couch with great expectation. Tim would be home soon and she was eager to see his expression when he saw the decorating she had done.

Tim and Emily's relationship was still in a young enough stage that they missed each other dearly when Tim had to be out of town. Their relationship was something that each one nurtured in their own way, to keep it ever new and fresh, but it was not without its trials.

176

Emily usually greeted Tim at the door, and he was a little disappointed to find her on the couch. Tim was vaguely aware that the room seemed more bright and cheery than usual but he did not notice any specific detail that was different and made no comment. Now, Emily was equally disappointed.

They talked briefly about his work and travel and then Tim, having learned that Francesca was napping, asked Emily what she had been up to. He was tired, and his tone was misinterpreted by Emily, who thought he was implying that she had spent the whole time on the sofa just lounging around. She responded, "Oh, nothing much," as she rolled her eyes around the room as a hint. The hint went as unnoticed as the decorating changes however and Tim went outside to fetch in some fuel for the woodstove. A chilly night was in the forecast. Indeed, a chill was already being felt in the house.

On the way through the garage he found a paint can and spilled paint on his workbench. As he walked past the chicken coop, a small, green, plastic cylinder caught his eye. He picked it up and put it in his pocket, muttering to himself, "What's going on around here?"

Upon returning to the house, he found Emily still sitting where he had left her. "What's going on around here?" he asked as he removed the spent .410 shell from his pocket. "Oh, that. I had a raccoon get into the chicken coop last night," answered Emily shyly. "You shot it?" questioned Tim with some astonishment. He had no idea that Emily was paying attention when Uncle Henry had demonstrated the use of the gun. Again, his tone was misread by an unusually sensitive Emily. She replied defensively, "Yes I shot it. What else was I to do? Leave it in there to ravage my flock?"

"Well, what's with the paint spilled on my workbench?" said Tim, not comprehending what paint had to do with shooting raccoons. "I painted the entire living room while you were gone. Apparently that was a waste of time since you didn't even notice."

Now the situation was becoming clear to Tim. He had neglected to notice and acknowledge Emily's work. Taking for

177

granted, the efforts of the spouse, seems a common pitfall in marriage and Tim was suddenly aware of his failure to communicate how much he did appreciate Emily's contribution.

He said, rather meekly, "Wasn't it brown before?" "It was never *brown,* it was Antique Brass and I painted it Harvest Gold, at least three shades lighter, and I patched up some nail holes and fixed that small crack near the ceiling and hung a new picture and rearranged the furniture..." Emily stopped there but her tone suggested that there was more that she could add.

They were both tired and knew it. And they were both realizing that the subject matter of their little argument was not significant in the grand scheme of things. As it happened, Francesca came to the rescue. "Listen. I hear Francesca fussing upstairs," said Emily, "why don't you go to her and I'll fix dinner. We'll get to bed early and tomorrow we'll both be in a better mood I suspect."

Emily was right. The next day she apologized for being so sensitive and Tim told her about his visit to his friend's house and how cold and sterile it seemed compared to their home. He apologized for not articulating his appreciation of her efforts. They shared a make-up kiss and then Tim asked, "What did you do with the dead raccoon anyway?" "Oh, I put it in the freezer. Butch is going to pick it up and make a coonskin cap." "It's in the freezer?! With the food that we are going to eat? You put a dead raccoon in our freezer?" The mush and sentiment of the moment was obliterated by the frozen carcass. Emily replied defensively, "Well, what else is in there? Dead cow, dead pig, dead fish." "Yeah, but those don't have the fur and claws still on," pointed out Tim with disgust.

Neither one of them wanted to ruin their day with another argument, so a compromise was reached when Tim declared it was a beautiful day for a drive and that maybe they should deliver the frozen goods to Butch. This was an agreeable solution to Emily, and so the storm passed without serious damage.

In August, Tim, Emily, and Francesca returned to the Hideaway and the Jack Pine. Harold, Lorraine, and Tricia, had their usual White Pine, but Jim, Elizabeth and Liz had switched to the Birch, anticipating the need for more room in future years as their family grew.

It was exciting to share this special place with their daughter and both Tim and Emily looked forward to seeing everything fresh through her eyes.

They enjoyed another week of swimming, boating, campfires, shopping, and just a celebration of family in a relaxing setting.

Emily decided to keep a scrapbook of their week at the lake. It included such items as a colored maple leaf from the tree that often turned very early, a wild turkey feather, some dried wild flowers, a butterfly wing, daily journal entries and notes, and of course, pictures. Tim's favorite was a picture of Francesca with Lucky the resort chicken.

The lone hen was dubbed: "Lucky" by some guests, earlier in the summer. It was the only chicken to survive raids from various predators; raccoon, fox, and mink for sure. Lucky was allowed to roam around for safety's sake and to seek companionship as best it might, and so, it developed a habit of mooching snacks from the guests, most of whom didn't seem to mind, anyway, the picture was awfully darn cute.

On the last full day of their vacation, Friday, Emily decided to take a walk around the resort while Tim and Francesca were napping. As she walked, her senses were more acute than usual and she seemed to absorb everything with a sense of urgency, as if her return was an uncertainty.

She stood on the end of a dock for some time. Seagulls, clouds, mallards. The weathered wood, warmed by the sun, felt good on her bare feet. The air had a pleasant, fresh smell like a breath across a blooming flower.

A humming bird and a bumblebee were busy about their work amongst the wild flowers that grew in front of the office. White and purple phlox seemed to be the main attraction.

As she walked along the edge of the pond, Emily felt, strangely, that there was a more than usual permanence to her departure this year. She watched a blue jay feather float by, a snail, grateful for the gift of a fallen tree branch, a leopard frog hopping through the tall green grass, carp, sunning themselves near the water's surface.

Further along, Emily saw a tree infested with tent caterpillars. She tried to get a closer look, but was menaced by black locust thorns and decided it probably wasn't that interesting after all, and anyway, growing within reach were both elderberries and wild grapes. That is where Elizabeth found her. "I've been looking all over for you." "Well, I'm right here," replied Emily simply. "Dad wants to go put down our deposits for next year."

It was traditional for the two girls, (Tricia had no interest) to accompany their dad to the office at the end of the week each year. Even as a young girl, Emily found satisfaction in this process. It seemed to guarantee their return. This year, Emily had another reason, other than tradition, to go along. She and Tim had decided to request Cabin 1 (Spruce) next year if it was available. (She had heard that the family that was in that cabin this year was coming back earlier next year.)

Harold, despite earning a smaller salary than either Tim or Jim, insisted on paying the deposits on their cabins. The girls thanked him with heartfelt hugs, and so, the reservations were made, but without the usual level of affirmation that Emily had come to expect.

That evening, after the boat was trailered and the traditional sister prepared dinner dishes cleaned up, Emily asked Tim if he was sure he didn't have any misgivings about switching cabins. "No, I'm looking forward to getting back into the old cabin. What about you, you've been sort of quiet today?" "Have I?" replied Emily, glad that Tim was paying attention, but disappointed that her inner discord was evident to others. "I guess you're right. Usually this week plays out like a piece of beautiful music. But this year there is discord. It's like someone has changed the time signature. The tempo is wrong. I'm an

180

octave off but I don't even know if I'm too high or too low. I keep playing a C sharp when I should play D." This analogy was made with a degree of hope in her voice but after a brief pause she concluded with complete solemnity, "Or maybe the instrument is out of tune."

On Monday, following their vacation, Emily made an appointment to see a doctor. Later that night, she told Tim about the appointment. He looked alarmed. "It's probably nothing, but I've had a recurring pain for a long time and it seems to be getting more frequent. I want to have it checked out, just as a precaution," said Emily. "You mean the pain that you told me about last year? You're still having that?" questioned Tim with disbelief. "Well, it comes and goes. Sometimes I forget about it for a month or two, then it comes back. Lately, it has been pretty bad though," finished Emily with a hint of resignation.

In a café on the outskirts of a small town, the type of café that, if it had been moved to any number of other small towns, it would have looked perfectly suited to that location, and appear to have been there since it's founding, sat a salesman, the very same character to which you have already been introduced.

Bill set his coffee cup down on the chrome edged, formica covered, booth table and watched as a waitress stepped lightly across the red and white checkered floor. She delivered an order to a couple sitting in another booth with a small child in a high chair. Bill smiled as he thought about his son, daughter-in-law, and one year old granddaughter.

Bill had spent most of his life on the road. A cheap hotel and small café were surroundings as familiar to him as a spring fed pond would be to a painted turtle. Yet, travel was becoming increasingly burdensome to him now that he had a granddaughter who was growing up so fast.

Francesca was like a new lens through which to view the world, a lens through which everything appeared fresh and new and full of wonder. Watching Francesca's reaction to things he had long since taken for granted gave him a new perspective.

In Francesca's innocent, uncorrupted world, events unfolded at a slower pace. There was a sequenciality to her day that seemed more an alternative to time than a function of it.

The waitress was summoned for the purpose of refilling Bill's coffee cup and as she poured the lifeblood of the traveling salesman, she asked how things were going and where he was headed and made agreeable small talk.

A café, such as the one Bill was dining in, is often populated with at least a few lonesome souls and a good waitress can perform her job as a ministry if she chooses. This waitress did, and she looked on with genuine interest as Bill showed her pictures of his son's family.

While he was eating his bowl of vegetable beef soup, (Emily had suggested that he needed to eat more vegetables) his cell phone rang.

Now Bill Vincy, being in the business that he was in, had always been on the cutting edge of the forefront of cell phone technology. When mobile phones were first introduced, and they looked more like a large World War II walkie-talkie, Bill had one. Brandishing one of those back in the day, in a café such as this, would start rumors about his being a CIA agent, drug smuggler, movie producer, Lieutenant Governor, or maybe even a Russian spy. Bill loved the attention, but there was a practical aspect of being connected that sometimes gave him an advantage over his competition. I'm imagining a salesmen version of Mad Magazine's Spy vs Spy when Bill went into an electronics store to upgrade his phone.

Bill considered himself a regular aficionado when it came to music. He listened to a lot of it on the road. In his attic sat a dusty box of 8 track tapes and next to that was a somewhat less dusty box of cassette tapes. The cassettes were retired when he bought a new car with a cd player in it. His cd collection was still on a shelf in the living room but these were seldom used since he now had most of his music stored on his phone. He had purchased some of his favorite albums four times in different formats.

Bill had recently switched his ring tone from "Planet Caravan" (Black Sabbath) to "Into Dust" by Mazzy Star. Bill interrupted lead singer Hope Sandoval's divine voice to answer it after noticing the call had originated from Tim's phone.

The conversation was brief, but what it lacked in duration, it made up for in intensity. After the phone was more or less allowed to drop to the table, Bill sat motionless until his soup and coffee were tepid, an unappealing temperature for any consumable liquid to be, that's for certain, but Bill's appetite had vanished along with any color that had been apparent in his face.

Suddenly roused from his trance by a soft touch on his arm from the vigilant waitress, Bill looked up. "Is anything wrong?" she asked with a hint of alarm at seeing his face, as white as Moby Dick. He answered in a weary, resigned tone, "My daughter-in-law has cancer."

The waitress sat right down next to Bill and they talked earnestly for a few minutes until she had to go take another order. Before she left, however, she looked straight at Bill, looked him straight in the eye, and said firmly, "You need to be strong. Your son is going to need you."

That little speech inspired in Bill a willingness to fight on. He finished his cold soup, left his coffee and a generous tip, and drove for home.

Chapter 13 Emily

After being released from the hospital, Emily was sent home, and the Brooke family rallied around her cause. Lorraine left Milwaukee, with solemn assurances from Elizabeth that Harold would be well fed, and traveled to Stillwater to care for Emily and help with Francesca. Jim drove her up and went back the same day. Despite her habit of monitoring Harold's driving, Lorraine was deathly afraid to drive long distances on her own.

Tricia and Bill had already worked out a schedule that would allow one or the other of them to be always at the house, but were greatly relieved when Lorraine arrived. Lorraine's presence had a calming effect on everyone involved.

She had a way of taking charge of a domestic situation, without any fuss or fanfare. Lorraine just did what needed to be done with such precision and confidence that others would ask her if she needed help or ask what to do next, and so, she would end up supervising in her own quiet way.

Henry, Portia, Amy, and even Steve were available for any little thing that needed doing.

A crisis can bring out the best in all of us if we respond selflessly.

If the meaning of life is to experience comfort and pleasure to the highest possible degree, then, I suppose, our lives, and their accompanying hardships, have no real purpose. But if the universe is a stage on which we have been placed for the purpose of making choices, then a crisis represents an opportunity to develop character, an opportunity to give without expectation of reciprocity, an opportunity to be molded and shaped into citizens worthy to dwell in that community of self-giving love and receptivity that Emily hoped for.

Molding and shaping a human being is a complex process that requires patience and perseverance, but hardening ourselves to change, refusing to let go of the material things we cling to, hinders the process and leads to anxiety, frustration, even despair.

Every morning, Emily would put on clothing as if she were waiting to be picked up by Tricia for a shopping excursion, or going out to pull weeds in the garden, or, in her case, harvest weeds in the garden. Then she would crawl back in bed, exhausted from the effort. She liked to be alone most of the time when she was sick, always had.

Tim would ask if she needed anything, a glass of water perhaps? She would respond no, she just needed some rest. Then five minutes later he would see her shuffling to the kitchen for a glass of water.

About a week after Emily had returned home, Tim looked in at his stricken bride, in the evening, as she was resting with Francesca.

It was a tranquil scene as the setting sun filtered into the room casting its soft shadows and illuminating the furnishings with a reddish orange glow.

Emily was gazing lovingly at her daughter. Her cheeks, which had been bereft of color those past several days, had a healthy luminescence about them.

Tim stole quietly into the room and sat on the edge of the bed. He saw the familiar fire in her eyes and a faint smile form at the corners of her mouth as he sat, but her gaze remained fixed on their child.

"You're going to get through this," he whispered with a conviction that rendered hope superfluous. Still watching

Francesca, Emily ventured a response, "I think so too," and she shifted her brown eyes, still fresh from the motherly adoration of her child, toward Tim, unleashing in him a rush of emotion.

There was an initial feeling of dread that he could be wrong, that was quickly washed away by a tender attraction, a desire to add to his family, and a sobering recollection that Emily could not have more children.

Emily's perceptive gaze had been studying Tim and she seemed to understand what he was thinking. Her eyes, as large as Tim had ever seen them, as brown, as white, moistened, and glistened with a single tear that ran down her cheek. Her smile slowly faded and she turned back to Francesca.

Tim's attention focused on a single purpose; to solve the problem, to repair the damage, fix what was broken. His mind raced, searching for the words to console his wife. "We could adopt," he heard himself saying almost before he even knew he had the idea.

Emily's smile returned.

The two young lovers talked about future plans, an activity which is sure to strengthen bonds in any two human beings, but especially effective when one is feeling vulnerable.

Making future plans, however, is a treacherous endeavor, for the future, it seems, is built on the shifting sands of free will. A computer program filled with If-Then-Go To statements. A web of contingencies based on the choices and decisions of ourselves, and others.

Emily had to return to the hospital often for treatments and follow up appointments of one sort or another. Bill and Tricia usually provided the transportation, but on a Friday in July, Tim had taken the day off from work and was driving Emily to an early morning appointment.

The county highway, that separated Tim and Emily's home from the hospital, took them past a decades-old establishment called the Sunbeam Tavern.

The Sunbeam was a popular watering hole with the third shift workers from the window factory because it was open early in the morning, to accommodate the 11 to 7 shift.

The air was clear that day, not a cloud to be seen and not the least trace of haze or fog to diminish the brightness of the sun, which at that time of day, was at a particularly offensive angle for anyone trying to drive, and see where they were going, if they were traveling east. Tim was driving west.

As he approached the Sunbeam, he noticed a car, coming from the opposite direction, with a left turn signal indicating the driver intended to turn into the Sunbeam parking lot.

The oncoming car began to turn into Tim's lane and he swerved right to avoid a collision but the other car just kept turning left and struck the rear quarter of Tim and Emily's vehicle.

At 45 miles per hour, this, in itself, would not have been a lethal exchange of kinetic energy, but the impact caused Tim's car to slide sideways into an electrical pole, caving in the passenger side door where Emily sat.

Tim and Francesca were unharmed, but Emily had to be extracted by emergency responders. A piece of metal had become lodged in her abdomen.

The awful sound of the crash haunted Tim's memory for some time. Crunched metal and shattering glass combined with the smell from the discharged air bags were sensations not easily forgotten. The smoke, or powder, from the air bags, was incorrectly interpreted by Tim as resulting from an engine compartment fire and he immediately turned to Francesca, who was facing backwards in her car seat, and crying, but otherwise unhurt.

He reached back, unfastened her from the front seat, and gently lifted her over, calling to Emily to get out quickly. He was unaware of the extent of her injury at first.

Patrons spilled out of the Sunbeam to offer assistance. In the confusion, Tim placed Francesca in the outstretched arms of someone, and hearing that an ambulance was on the way, turned to see why Emily was not getting out.

It was then that he saw the blood issuing from her wound. He tore off his shirt and applied gentle pressure in an attempt to slow the loss of blood. Emily was in shock.

After stabilizing her at the hospital, the emergency room doctor called Tim aside and explained the gravity of the situation. She had suffered damage to her internal organs, a specialist had been called in, surgery was needed, and with her weakened immune system, there was a high risk for infection.

Lorraine arrived at the hospital with Henry and Portia, just as Emily was being taken, unconscious, into the surgery room. Lorraine, seeing Emily's face, white from the loss of blood, and the outline of her emaciated body under a sheet, as she was rolled down the hallway, knew, with a sudden rush of awareness, the severity of her daughter's condition.

Lorraine sunk to the floor and with her back to the wall and her face hidden in her hands, cried angry, frightened, sorrowful tears. With the release of emotion, came some relief from the bitter anguish that she was feeling.

Tim and Tricia assured each other that she would pull through and did not allow the unthinkable thought to occupy their minds. They kept busy making phone calls, comforting Lorraine and Francesca, and questioning the doctors and nurses.

Harold and Elizabeth drove up from Milwaukee as soon as they heard the tragic news, and arrived at the hospital about the same time that Emily was being moved to intensive care.

The surgery was considered a success, much to the relief of the family, and after two days, Emily was moved from intensive care to a regular room. Everyone's hopes were lifted, but the next day, a high fever set in and complications were discovered. She had an infection and her weakened immune system was incapable of stopping the rapid growth of the malicious organism that had taken up residence in her frail body.

Emily was not bitter. She did have some anxiety about Tim and Francesca, but she had a plan for that, and suffered with heroic patience, the discomfort that the pain medication did not always control adequately.

At this time, the family saw in her eyes something that I cannot put into words adequately. How can I describe the indescribable? So much sadness but at the same time so much hope.

I witnessed recently, a dark, concentrated rain cloud blow over Lake Wissota. The sun pierced through the fringes of it and shafts of light illuminated the drops of rain as they fell. Two miles away, they did not get any rain, but it fell hard where I was. As it passed over, a perfect arch became visible, red, orange, yellow, green, blue, indigo, and violet. It spanned from some mysterious point on land and terminated in the middle of the lake.

The lake has a mood and a personality of its own, reflecting the color of the sky, yes, but equally affected by the wind. It can change with an astonishing suddenness.

Emily's eyes reflected the inner colors, blue, indigo, violet. An unknown force, powerful enough to sever a rainbow, suppressed her hope, only allowing a ray to escape here and there. There is a mysterious loneliness to pain. Even those close to you do not know. An intense gust, a razor sharp glare.

For a few days, Emily fought on and the antibiotics seemed to be working, but on the fourth day after the infection was discovered, Tim received a call from Emily's doctor. Family members were summoned to her bedside. The high fever had returned and the doctors were left with little or no options.

For about an hour, the family talked quietly and prayed as Emily drifted in and out of consciousness.

By and by, Emily lifted her head weakly in order that she might peer through half open eyes at her family, gathered around her bed. Seeing her Beth at the bedside, she grasped her hand, closed her eyes, and allowed her head to rest back into the pillow, whispering, "I'd like to be alone with Tim."

As the family filtered out of the room, Tricia glanced back and noticed that Emily was retaining Elizabeth. Tricia felt a tinge of pain at seeing this. She had never been jealous of Elizabeth and it was not jealousy that she felt now. Perhaps a sense that she had not earned Emily's trust or demonstrated enough maturity to be included in her confidence would account for what she was feeling. Elizabeth looked forlornly back at Tricia,

"What can I do, she has hold of my hand," her expression seemed to say.

Speech came with no little effort and as Emily gathered strength, she thought out carefully the words she would say to Tim. "If I die, you have my blessing to marry Tricia," was the urgent message she needed to convey, but when Tim and Elizabeth leaned close, Emily heard herself say in a barely audible whisper, "I want you to marry Trish."

Tim tearfully uttered the obligatory remonstrations that she would pull through and such things as you can imagine he would say, while Elizabeth gave silent consideration to the task that had been assigned her.

As Emily relaxed from the effort of communication, the placid softness returned to her eyes. The winds died down and the smooth water again reflected the sun that was setting with a beautiful display of red, orange, yellow, and green.

Emily slipped peacefully into a state of unconsciousness with a barely discernible smile on her thin lips. Her breathing gradually slowed over the next few hours, and with her family at her side, she breathed her last.

As her mortal body was separated from the animating power of her soul, a small child was left to face a cold world without the guidance and reassuring embrace of a mother.

As that last breath of warm moist air entered Emily's lungs, tethers and anchor lines were severed and her last exhalation unintentionally filled the sails of two vessels and cast them adrift on a vast and forbidding psychological ocean that was disturbingly devoid of stability, composure, and balance.

As that childlike gleam of hope and wonder in Emily's eyes, faded to black, a sister, who despite the pain she was experiencing, now faced the responsibility of lashing those two vessels securely together, that they might ride out the storm as one, and this mission would have to be fulfilled while carrying the additional burden of consoling two broken-hearted parents.

The End

Tricia Vincy sat on the end of the dock, gazing intently at a small white object halfway across the lake. A seagull was floating lazily, its color sharply contrasting the deep blue of the water that reflected the late afternoon sky in mid August.

On the boat lift near her was a 1960 Inland Lakes boat in which a small child was playing and waiting impatiently to feed breadcrumbs to that seagull and any others that might happen to be hanging about. The small child was both her niece and her adopted daughter. Time was gradually eroding the bitter aspect of that bittersweet arrangement.

She sat musing on the tower of strength, kindness and courage that she had lost, no longer grieving, but remembering so as not to be forgetting. Emily's presence had been the lighthouse that she had so often sought, to find her way to the shores of equanimity, when she was tossed about on the seas of her restlessness, her reassurance when the froth and foam of shame and doubt formed and swirled on the cresting waves of her anxiety.

Tricia knew that Tim's life had also been changed by this demanding, patient, fiercely loyal, gentle creature that had graced their lives. Emily, in whom there was to be found no duplicity.

Presently, Timothy sat down next to Tricia. She took his hand in hers and placed it on her rounded belly. "Do you feel a kick?" she asked as she looked at him serenely. Tim just smiled and nodded affirmatively.

He put his arm around her then, and she leaned her head against his shoulder. And so they sat in silence, like two wandering stars that had been saved from the blackness of darkness, and set aright, to shine as one, from the heavens.